The Incident
Copyright © 2020 Richard B. Christie

Library of Congress Control Number	2020922785
Paperback	978-1-63626-072-3
Hardcover	978-1-63626-073-0
eBook	978-1-63626-074-7

Printed in the United States of America

PaperChase
S O L U T I O N

Harrison Street, Hoboken
New Jersey, 07030
www.paperchase-solution.com
+1-800-850-2688

THE
INCIDENT

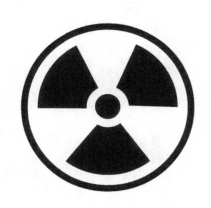

RICHARD B. CHRISTIE

This book is dedicated to all United States Veterans,
who are currently serving, or have served in the past.

Thank you and may God bless you.

Table of Contents

PROLOGUE

A cold and cloudy January day became very uncomfortable for the sailors aboard a Russian nuclear submarine, the Nikolayevich Kosinski. They were forced to surface only two miles north of Atka Island, located in the American Aleutian Chain of Islands, in the southern portion of the Bering Sea.

Uncomfortable because they were in United States territorial waters and they weren't supposed to be; and were frightened because they had developed a catastrophic radioactive leak that had forced all those aboard to close off the ship's whole aft end.

It quickly became an international embarrassment that required assistance from the United States Coast Guard, the United States Navy, and even several American commercial fishermen.

First, they had to rescue the Russian sailors; luckily, all survived.

Then, with the arrival and aid of two Russian support ships, they towed the contaminated submarine to a location in the northern part of the Bering Sea, where they could scuttle it in five thousand feet of water. It is a very remote, deep, and isolated location where it can do no more harm.

It proved to be an extraordinary joint cooperative effort between the Russian and United States governments. It was unusual that they both could put politics aside and fix the problem before it got out of hand.

Of course, there would be discussions and some uncomfortable reporting in the world news that would try to escalate the situation; still, this time, it was too clear of a problem, and the obvious corrective solution was inevitable.

The surviving Russian sailors were transferred to one of the Russian support ships and returned home without further incident.

CHAPTER ONE

Tuesday, 19 March 2019
Northwest District Apartments
Washington D.C.

L ieutenant Jane McCalla, an investigator at the Naval Special Investigation Unit (NSIU), sat in her apartment and thought about all that had happened over the last few years. Her birthday was next Tuesday, she was going to turn twenty-seven-years-old, and now, she needed to make a huge career choice.

She had grown up in a little suburb of Louisville, Kentucky, and was the only child of two parents who were both lawyers. Her mother was appointed a district judge twelve years ago, and her father was the head of a fair-sized Law firm with a strong reputation for fairness.

Jane graduated from High School with honors, when she turned eighteen, and immediately applied to Kentucky University. Upon her acceptance, and over the next four years, she studied for a Bachelor of Science degree in advanced mathematics, with a minor in psychology.

The two paths of study gave her the ability to form logical answers to complex problems. It was her primary advanced math professor, a woman named Sally Martin, who, during two semesters, could see there was a bright future for her top student.

Jane, a very resourceful young woman, decided to join the military instead of following her parents' wishes to continue onto Law School. She had inherited a stubbornness from her father. It manifested itself only three weeks after graduation; when she came home and told them, she had applied to the United States Navy Officer's Candidate School (OCS).

It wasn't that Jane disliked the law; after all, she has seen enough of it her whole life. But she had found she wanted a different challenge, one that would allow her the world travel she had longed for, and yet, felt a strong pull at her to be part of the United States Navy.

As her training at OCS in Newport, Virginia, was ending, a three-star admiral interviewed her. Vice-Admiral Harry Walker needed a junior officer to be an assistant for his small command in Washington, DC. The Admiral was the head of the NSIU.

As a commissioned officer on his staff three weeks later, Jane found herself in the nation's capital, as an Ensign in the U. S. Navy.

The NSIU was a small unit consisting of three officers, eight enlisted navy seals, two enlisted navy secretaries, and two civilian contract investigators. It was formed several years ago as an asset to the Department of Defense (DOD) and usually is assigned to special investigations and cases with significant international involvement.

Over the next few years, she found that although she wasn't at sea, her assigned shore duty was fascinating and essential. Somehow, the law that had been a major part of her whole life just seemed to continue.

After several important investigations, where she proved that the Admiral was correct in assessing her abilities, she was advanced in rank to Lieutenant JG, then recently on to full Lieutenant, a remarkable advancement in only a few years.

On several occasions, NSIU would also aid in a few FBI or CIA investigations, when requested by the Department of Justice (DOJ) or the State Department (DOS).

Just a few months ago, such a complex investigation of significant importance took place in Mexico. In this very elusive investigation, all the various agencies, working together, found a way to stop a potential major economic disaster. With the Mexican Army's help, they also were able to solve a terrible international murder case.

It was during these actions that Jane met the head investigator from the FBI, thirty-one-year-old Miguel Lôpez. He was the FBI agent in charge of the Mexican investigation. Soon both of them found that they were becoming attracted to each other romantically.

At the completion of the investigation closeout review meeting, Jane received an unusual request to please telephone Secretary of State Weiss over at DOS.

For a young lieutenant officer, it was a very strange request. But when she called him, he said to her: "Elizabeth has submitted her application for a change in position, and I will soon need a new 'State Department Spokesperson.'

"I have talked with Admiral Walker, and we both agree, and believe that you would be a good choice to fill that position. So, I ask, would you be willing to leave your current Navy position and move over to the State Department?"

That was the choice she had to make.

It was a much easier decision than she had first thought. The honor of being chosen as the official spokesperson of the United States State Department was truly great. After a few phone calls to her parents, and after a conversation with Admiral Walker, Jane placed a phone call to Miguel to tell him she would accept the position.

Friday, she was at her new office over at the State Department and was already taking notes on many of the conversations Secretary Weiss was having. Conversations that were possibly going to affect the world.

Her first news conference was to be the following Monday.

CHAPTER TWO

Monday, 25 March 2019
NSIU Headquarters
Washington D.C.

Admiral Harry Walker was at his desk looking at the daily briefings early on this bright and windy Monday morning. They had been in his lockbox as usual, and he was starting to read through them when Lieutenant Commander Harold Jarrett and Chief Petty Officer Paul DeNice entered his office.

He looked up at them and said: "Good morning, I just opened the lockbox, and you can help read through these with me. The coffee pot is already on, and hot, so help yourselves."

Paul and Harold smiled at the Admiral, went over to the pot, and poured themselves each a cup. Then, without asking, they each proceeded to steal a donut from the box alongside it.

As they sat down, the Admiral looked at the donuts in their hands and said: "I said coffee, you guys are going to owe me." Then with a sigh, said: "I should know better."

As they smiled at him and sipped their coffee, he handed them each a file, and they began to read the information of interest regarding current activities.

Paul looked up from the file in his hand and said: "Why is that there is almost always a comment about the crime wave in Chicago, doesn't the local government have any control?

"There was another attack on the federal courthouse grounds Saturday, and there was a shooting on the Southside again with three dead and five injured. I still don't know why we are always copied with these reports; they are all in the local province, not the DOD."

"I don't know Paul," said the Admiral, "but I think they hope there will be something we see, that they don't, that will let them solve this ongoing wave. It has so much political pushback that they are looking everywhere for a solution."

Harold said: "Moving along; there has been very little coverage regarding the Russian submarine incident by the Aleutian Islands about a month or so ago, but there are still many questions regarding it that we just don't know. I see that again; it is referred to in this weekend's reports. There is no further information, only the summary.

"What does DOD want us to do with this? It was handled properly by our Navy, and the Russian Navy, although embarrassed, remained cordial about it. Are they still wondering what the Russians were doing so close to our shore? Attached to the report is a request that we begin an inquiry into the explosion aboard their submarine. That is not something any of us have any idea about."

Admiral Walker sat back and said: "I haven't figured that out either. The Russians are frequently in the Bering Sea, but they seemed a little careless that time, and have paid a stiff penalty for it."

Perhaps DOD is just hopeful that we may have stumbled onto a reason that they may have missed. But, since they have now assigned us to begin an investigation, see if you can develop a plan.

Harold said: "I don't even know where to begin with this, have you any ideas?"

Responding, the Admiral said: "Other than to start with the various scientific agencies, including NASA, the Atomic Energy Commission (AEC), and whoever else you can think of, I suggest that you pick Paul and a couple of available team members and start down at the Norfolk Naval Center."

Then, leaning forward again, he picked up the last file and said: "Things are getting a little hot again in Iran, this time it is the local citizens that are creating a problem for their government. There were riots in Tehran last night, and we have word that the Swiss embassy was closed up, so there was no place for the rioters to go for shelter.

"It is good information, but I have no idea why it is in our lockbox.

"I will contact someone over at DOD and see if they have any idea why we are on the need to know list for this?"

Pushing his chair back from his desk, leaning back and smiling, he added: "I heard from Secretary Weiss that Jane is going to hold her first press conference at eleven o'clock this morning, and she will be taking questions."

Then looking at Paul and Harold, he said: "I would like to show her that we will always have her back. So, I thought that it might be nice if you, Paul, maybe in civilian clothes, and with Linda, could both be in the press room when she gives her report. I can call over to the Secretary's office to get you 'press' passes.

"Just don't bust on any reporter that hits her with a stupid 'gotcha' question. She can handle them, but I think it would be a boost for her just to know you are there."

As Paul got up to leave, he said: "Great idea, I'll go find Linda and let her know we are going to attend Jane's first 'Press Conference.' Then, maybe we can all go for lunch at O'Rourke's Irish Pub; do you want to meet us there?"

The Admiral answered: "Sounds like a good plan. Give us a call when you leave the DOS."

As they left the Admiral's office, Harold said to him: "You know, I think I should call Sally (Congresswoman Sally Martin) and ask her to join us for lunch as well. After all, Sally was Jane's math professor, and they've been close friends."

Paul responded: "Good idea if you can give her a call; I'll see if I can find Linda."

Linda DeSanto had been a Sergeant in the Vermont State Police when a curious murder case involved the NSIU. Her participation, cooperation, and professionalism, in that case, led to the Admiral offering her a position as a contract investigator, and she has been in Washington ever since.

Paul found her in the break room, reading the morning news and drinking coffee. As he joined her at the table, he said: "There probably isn't much value in that newspaper; lately there is too much-unrelated reporting that slants the story in favor of the editor's opinion."

"I know," said Linda, "But if you put aside their slant, at least you know something has happened; and then you can look elsewhere for facts that describe the real situation."

Paul shrugged and said: "I suppose so! Anyway, I just left the Admiral's office, and he mentioned that today at eleven o'clock, Jane would be having her first press briefing over at State. He thinks we should support her and let her know we have her 'Six.' So, he asked if you and I would go over to the press room at State and sit in on her briefing to show that we are looking out for her."

"I love the idea," said Linda, "Jane should do very well. I haven't got anything on my schedule, that can't wait, so I'm in."

Paul continued: "Then the Admiral said we could all have lunch over at O'Rourke's so we can tell them how Jane made out. Harold said he would call Sally and see if she can join us there."

CHAPTER THREE

Monday, 25 March 2019
U.S. State Department
Press Conference Room

Almost six weeks after the disastrous loss of their submarine, the Nikolayevich Kosinski, the Russian head of naval operations, was still trying precisely to determine what had happened in the Bearing Sea.

When the surviving crew members arrived and were immediately sent to the hospital for evaluation and confinement, there had been little time to interview them and find the cause. However, after primary medical evaluation, the Captain was removed and placed in confinement, where the experts from Moscow could look into everything he knew.

They were not too upset that the Americans were there to contain the situation, for it had been a serious breach for the sub to even be in American waters, and ultimately the Captain would be the one to pay the price.

However, it was the cause of the radioactive contamination that had them concerned. All that had been determined was that there had been an explosion in the primary reactor bay. They had not determined the cause of the explosion; on the contrary, the reactor bay was the least likely location of an explosion on the ship. However, not only was there an explosion in the bay, but it had been determined that the top of the reactor itself had been the place where the damage was most severe.

Since the last time it was in for routine service, the record of the submarine's activities, and all ports of call, was in the Captain's log. He had taken it off the ship when the rescue took place and kept it on his person the whole time. The Americans knew he had the record in his possession, but they did not try to take it from him in an unusual show of respect.

It had been a little over four months ago when they were last in Vladivostok, and the records kept at the naval headquarters in Moscow showed the same files and activities as were written in his log.

The Russians have about sixty total submarines, twenty-seven of them nuclear powered, and the rest conventional diesel-electric. They have not added much to their fleet since the end of the cold war, so most of their atomic boats are well past twenty-five years of age. The Nikolayevich Kosinski was commissioned in 1992 and used primarily in the North Pacific and the Bering sea.

The American Secretary of State, and his team, had visited Moscow last month and had many questions regarding the incident.

Although it was a closed case regarding the necessary actions that had taken place, Secretary Weiss was very concerned about the nuclear reactor's failure. The explosion, occurring in the near-coastal location, had forced the significant cooperative effort that was needed to secure a safe result.

The discussions regarding the reason for the Nikolayevich Kosinski to be in American waters were almost laughable. The Russians stated that it had been the Captain's actions, after the explosion, that had forced him to head towards the nearest shore, which just happened to be on Atka Island, while he was having his crew seal off the contaminated area.

Secretary Weiss's team ignored the obvious lie and made no further comment. They knew that the Russians were constantly off North America's coast, usually trying to monitor any actions or communications where Americans were involved. They also knew that all Russian, or for that matter, Chinese or any other potential naval threat, was always closely shadowed. The American Navy's fleet of very superior nuclear submarines and surface vessels knew exactly when anyone crossed into or was near American territorial waters.

The fact that the U. S. Navy and the U. S. Coast Guard were on the scene so quickly was a sign that they immediately knew what was happening.

The answer as to the cause of the explosion remained unknown and was a big concern for everyone involved. It would be discussed on the floor of the United Nations and the International Atomic Energy Commission. Unusual as it was, the Russians were also looking for answers and agreeing to listen to any input.

When the Americans were back in Washington, Secretary Weiss sent an urgent request to the DOD, asking them to look into any possible way the submarine's reactor bay could explode without intervention or help from some human source. The conversations they had in Moscow were beginning to make them believe that someone involved wanted such a serious event to happen. That brings up the question of who, and even more critical, why?

It seemed that the Russian submarine incident was the primary source of interest for the DOS, but it was only one item on a full plate.

Back at DOS in Washington, as Secretary Weiss and his advisors went over the multitude of issues that needed attention, Jane sat quietly at the conference table with her notebook. She was busy keeping detailed notes regarding what can and cannot be released to the public. She had learned from her time at NSIU that information was frequently confusing if not carefully explained or researched.

The items she would address this morning included:

- An update on the Russian submarine negotiations,

- the riots in Tehran over the weekend,

- arguments involving diplomats that were being discussed in the House of Representatives,

- the potential need for an election of a new Prime Minister in a small African country, and

- the appointment confirmation of a new ambassador.

After the early morning conference, Jane sat alone with Secretary Weiss and went over his thoughts regarding the topics she would be telling the press at eleven o'clock.

Since this was Jane's first news conference, the Secretary said he would be available, but not in the press room. If she needed him, she had a small pager button that she could use to call him, and he would come right in.

At eleven o'clock, Jane entered the press room and stepped up to the podium. After looking around at the dozen or so reporters, she smiled at two very special people sitting in the back of the room. Jane felt a surge of pride when she saw Paul and Linda; just knowing they were there was very reassuring.

Again, looking across the room, Jane said: "Good morning, my name is Jane McCalla; and for those of you who haven't heard, Elizabeth has moved to a new position as an assistant attaché in the United Kingdom.

Secretary Weiss asked if I would take the responsibility of reporting to you the State Department's current events and concerns.

"First, to tell you a little about me, I have served in the United States Navy for the past few years as a Lieutenant assigned to the Naval Special Investigation Unit. As part of that unit, I have been an active investigator on several international cases and incidents at the State Department's request.

"So, I ask you to please, give me a chance to know and get used to each of you, and for you to know and get used to me."

A mild murmur in the room had the effect of relaxing Jane as she began her presentation regarding the State Department's current events. Over the next twenty minutes, Jane, occasionally looking at her notes, described the many current international events of interest to the public.

On the dais, alongside her notes, a diagram of the press room showed each reporter's name and news service's location. So, after finishing the comprehensive report, she said: "If you have any questions, please raise your hand, state your name, and I'll do my best to answer them."

Silence in the room lasted for about five seconds, and then three hands shot up with voices tripping over each other as they tried to get her attention.

Jane put up her hand and said with a strong, firm voice: "Stop! I said, raise your hand, and I will call upon you; shout out like that, and I promise that I'll ignore you completely."

Paul and Linda could hardly hold their laughter inside themselves at that comment from Jane; obviously, none of the reporters knew her, or they would know better.

Jane had regained complete control of the room, and the few questions that followed were courteous and reasonable for the most part.

After closing the conference, Jane wrote a short note and asked for an aid to please give it to Paul or Linda as they were getting ready to leave. The note was short and sweet; it said, 'Please get me the hell out of here and take me to lunch!'

CHAPTER FOUR

Monday, 25 March 2019, 12:45 p.m.
O'Rourke's Irish Pub
New Jersey Avenue, NW
Washington, D.C.

As they were leaving the State Department, Paul put in a call to Admiral Walker and told him they would be at O'Rourke's at a quarter to one and that Jane was coming with them.

When Linda, Jane, and Paul walked in, there was mild applause from the Admiral, Harold, and Sally. To everyone's surprise, except the Admiral, two minutes later, Secretary of State Weiss himself walked in, handed Jane a bouquet of roses, and said to her as he sat down: "You did a superb job, I am so pleased to have you on our team."

For the second time in just a few months, both times when she was with the Secretary, Jane had nothing to say. She was flattered by her new boss's attention and honored by the presence of her friends from NSIU.

It was Linda, who was the first one to say: "Jane, you were great! I think that silly reporter from NNN will think twice before he ever asks you another 'gotcha' question.

Secretary Weiss said: "I watched you on the TV and knew almost at once that you were in complete control of those reporters.

"Oh! And Elizabeth called from London and said she watched you live on BBC and thinks that you were just great."

After regaining control, Jane said: "Thank you all, it is a huge change for me, and I didn't know if I could handle it. Mr. Secretary, I will do my very best to show you that you have a spokesperson who will get the information out as it should be; and I promise not to kill any reporter no matter how revolting they may become!"

As they all laughed together, Jane knew that she had all the support and backup she would ever need.

After a good Irish luncheon, they each headed back to their own offices at both the DOS and the NSIU.

Back at the NSIU, Harold asked the Admiral if he and Paul could sit and discuss what he learned from his DOD conversation. He said: "They believe that it is highly unlikely that the Nikolayevich Kosinski explosion was accidental. It is almost impossible for that type of explosion to blast the outside of the reactor cover and open it to a radioactive leak, without something highly explosive being placed directly in contact with that cover.

"In a statement from our AEC group in Utah, they say that even though the Russian nuclear facilities aren't up to the same standards as we are, they absolutely know what they are doing. In other words, they are saying it obviously wasn't an accident."

Paul said: "If it isn't an accident, then someone did it deliberately. The question, therefore, is who and why? Additionally, why was it done in such proximity to the United States, albeit on a Russian ship?"

The Admiral sat quietly thinking, and after about a minute said: "OK, we need to find out! Harold, who on our team is available for the next few weeks?"

With a questioning look at Paul, Harold said: "I don't know, Paul, do you?"

Paul answered: "Well, outside of you, me, and Linda, I think most are on assignment or unavailable.

"Chief Ira Jones should be back by the end of the week; he is on leave in Western Canada. The rest of our seal team six: Luigi Larenti, Antonio Romani, David Likus, John McCall, Peter Dove, and Rudy O'Neil are all finishing up with that new seal cold weather refresher course up in Kodiak, Alaska; they should all be back here by Thursday night.

"We haven't yet tried to replace Carl Muskin after he left active duty and married Lijuan last winter. But he is back teaching a history course at Central Texas University. Although unavailable, I understand he is keeping up with his reserve training time.

"Lonnie Carswell, our legal advisor, and other civilian contract research investigator, hasn't been involved with any field assignment in several years."

Harold, nodding, then said: "Right at the moment, it is just the four of us, including you, sir."

The Admiral, with an undeserved dirty look at both Paul and Harold, said with a sigh: "You forgot Seaman Jimmy Louis and Seaman Susan Gordon," then with his hand up to stop further comment, said: "I know they are our office clerks and we need them where they are."

Then with a smile, said: "OK, I need to find a replacement for Jane, we sure will miss her. I'll look into that, and you two, along with Linda, see if you can come up with a plan to find answers to the Sub's explosion's cause-and-effect."

Strange things happen every so often, and that afternoon was no different. The Admiral was sitting thinking about finding another young female officer who had the knowledge and integrity to be a valued part of his command.

Nothing was coming to mind, so, to give himself a short break, and with a sigh, he picked up his phone and placed a call to an old friend who was the head of the U. S. Coast Guard Officer's Candidate School in New London, Connecticut.

Rear-Admiral Billy Wicks had known Harry Walker since they were both in college together more than thirty years ago. Although Billy was in the Coast Guard, and Harry was in the Navy, they had remained friends for years and sent notes back and forth to each other frequently, usually downplaying each other's military choice with mild insults.

Today, however, when Billy answered, and after a brief exchange of insults, he took the opportunity to ask Harry for a favor. It seems that his nephew would graduate from medical school in a couple of months and wanted to intern somewhere near Washington, D.C.

Billy's family, all lived in New Jersey, and almost everyone he knew was from that area. So, he asked his friend if he knew anyone who could help his nephew find a doctor's resident position at Walter Reed, where he could become an intern for the needed time.

Harry said that he didn't know anyone specifically, but he had met the hospital's head several times, and although he didn't know him very well, he could give Billy his name and the direct phone number. Billy thanked him and asked how things were going at NSIU.

Harry told him that they were very busy, and now his chief aid, Lieutenant Jane McCalla, had been stolen from him by the State Department, as their new spokesperson. He was thinking about getting started looking for another young aid to replace her.

With a strange change of tone, Billy laughed and asked: "Does it need to be a woman?"

Harry said: "No, but I only have two women on my staff, one is a seaman secretary, and the other is a civilian contract investigator. We deal with many international connections, and frequently a woman's viewpoint is of great value. Also, a woman officer is frequently accepted in places where a male might have a problem."

Billy was quiet for a few moments and said: "You know, I have a young woman Lieutenant Commander, Connie Wall, who has been at the Academy for about seven years. She is thirty-two-years-old, brilliant, and quite capable. I think she might be someone who could work well with your people. Would it bother you that your assistant was a Coast Guard Officer instead of Navy?"

Harry laughed and said: "No, it wouldn't bother me at all, but how do you know she might be available, or would even want to change jobs?"

Billy, with a serious tone to his voice, answered, "She wanted to be a lawyer, but never had the support from her family. She never married, but remains very dedicated to whatever task we assign her. Our problem is that I don't have enough complex things here at the Academy to challenge her mind or abilities."

Harry, with a questioning tone, asked: "If I fly up there tomorrow, can I meet and interview her, without her knowing it is for a possible change in position?"

"I don't see why not," said Billy, "we are friends, and you could just be visiting me for lunch. I'll find some excuse so she will be available while you are here, and you can make your own judgment."

"OK," said Harry, "I'll see you about eleven o'clock tomorrow morning."

CHAPTER FIVE

Tuesday, 26 March 2019
United States Coast Guard
Officer's Candidate School
New London, Connecticut

Admiral Walker's Plane landed at the Coast Guard Academy at ten-forty-five Tuesday morning. As he was getting out, he was met by four Cadets who, under the watchful eye of their Unit Commander, were there to escort him to Billy's office. As he walked over to his office, it was obvious that his Navy-Blue uniform was a much darker blue than the Coast Guard's Service Dress Blues.

When he was shown into Billy's office, and after a friendly greeting, his opening comment was: "Billy, you need to find a better shelter for your people, their uniforms are bleached way too much from always being out in the sun!"

Billy, with a short snort, responded: "That is the difference between the Coast Guard and the Navy; we actually are on the water and exposed to the sun's reflection, whereas you and your people are always hiding inside and afraid to get your face tanned."

Harry, with a huge smile and a laugh, responded: "So it begins!"

Laughing, they walked out together and got into Billy's command car and were driven off the base on their way to the fishing pier in Mystic, with its famous lobster restaurant.

As they sat down at a quiet table near the window, looking out over the small fishing harbor and docks, both began to relax and ordered the house special, 'Fresh Lobster Roll on a Philadelphia Soft Bun.' Since they were the senior officers at the base, and no one would dare say anything, they both decided to have a nice cold beer along with it.

"So, tell me all about Lieutenant Commander Connie Wall, and why are you willing to give her up?" Asked Harry.

Billy said: "I don't want to give her up; on the contrary, I want her to stay where she is. But that wouldn't be fair to her.

"Connie is a very pleasant young woman, and she came to us from the Merchant Marine about seven years ago. I learned that she had graduated from the Merchant Marine Academy as a Third Officer (Mate).

After having been hired only six months, she was the third officer on a trans-Atlantic freighter. Her people skills had become obvious, and she was immediately transferred and made the Personnel Director for a large shipping company in New York, the one who owned the freighter.

"After three years, it had become obvious, to her, that they were using her position for mild documental tasks. So, when she turned twenty-five, she decided that she needed to make a change. She had always wanted to go on to Law School, but her family wasn't thrilled, and she couldn't afford it on her own.

"That was when she applied for a transfer to the Coast Guard as a commissioned officer. We were very glad to have her."

"So, what brought her to your command?" said Harry.

Billy said: "The notes in her record stated that although she held a Third Officer (Mate) commission in the Merchant Marine, there were several minor areas of difference to the Coast Guard officers program.

The idea was if she was assigned to the Coast Guard OCS, her officer status could remain, albeit as a Lieutenant, and she could easily become adept in our ways; while, at the same time, being an integral part of the program."

"I see," said Harry: "Has it worked out as planned?"

Billy responded, "Far better, she has a brilliant mind and, I have seen in her more patience than anyone I've ever known. I have seen her listen to comments and complaints from both Cadets, and even some of her associates, with total attention; then calm the storm with simple logical advice and reason. They all always seem to understand things and act better after they have talked with Connie."

Upon returning to the base, it was easy for Admiral Walker to meet and speak with Lieutenant Commander Connie Wall. As the two Admirals were walking across the field, they stopped to watch a small group of Cadets receiving instructions from her on proper arriving aircraft personnel reception etiquette.

By seeing the two Admirals standing there watching, she immediately used their presence as an example.

Standing at attention, she looked at Billy and, with a direct look from her eye, respectfully said: "May I, Admiral?"

Both with more than thirty years of military experience, Billy and Harry stood quietly relaxed as Billy answered: "Of course Lieutenant Commander."

With that authorization, Connie proceeded to have each of her Cadets follow the prescribed escort rules and procedures for arriving superior officers. It was a short instruction and, with two such senior officers there, a very powerful one.

As she finished her demonstration, she released her Cadets, and after they moved away, turned and saluted both Admirals and said: "Thank you, sir, they were having a little problem understanding the sequence."

At which point, Billy said: "Well done, Lieutenant Commander. Let me introduce Admiral Harry Walker from the United States Navy Special Investigation Unit, usually referred to as the NSIU.

"Admiral, this is Lieutenant Commander Connie Wall, one of our lead instructors."

Then with an unusually relaxed and friendly tone of voice, said: "Connie, why don't you join us for a short tour around the Academy. Actually, if you would please take the Admiral around for a few minutes, I need to make a quick stop and place an important call from my office. I'll catch back up with you."

Before anyone could respond, he nodded to Harry and walked away in the direction of his office.

Connie was dumbstruck, but Harry just couldn't hold in the laughter. He said: "Lieutenant Commander, please understand that I have known Admiral Wicks since we were in college together more than thirty years ago. He hasn't changed; come to think of it, neither have I. If you have the time, I would like to walk around and see your Academy. Please relax, and we can chat a bit."

With her military background, Connie recovered from the sudden change of events, smiled, nodded, and said: "Of course Admiral, I would be very honored to guide you around."

Over the next half hour, Harry, a very experienced investigator himself, was able to have Connie tell him everything he needed to know without her realizing that she was being interviewed.

When Billy caught up with them, he had a questioning look in his eye as he glanced at them.

Harry nodded and said: "Admiral, would you be very upset if I ask the Lieutenant Commander, here, if she would like to leave the world of military education and join my unit in Washington as an investigator and my assistant?"

The color completely drained from Connie's face, and, even in the presence of two such senior officers, her mouth just fell open!

Billy turned toward Connie and, in a very soothing voice, said: "Lieutenant Commander, please forgive our little deception, but Admiral Walker and I spoke of you and your future military career yesterday. He has come to New London today to have a chance to meet and interview you for the position he has just offered.

"We will apply no pressure upon you for an answer, and this is solely your decision."

Harry then said: "Admiral Wicks is correct; this decision is yours and yours alone. If you are inclined, I invite you to review the NSIU command, and over the remainder of this week, feel free to ask any questions you may have. I will provide you with our senior officer, Commander Harold Jarrett's direct line. He will answer any questions. However, we will need an answer from you by Friday."

With her acumen returned, Connie said: "Thank you sir, but I am in the Coast Guard, not the Navy."

With a smile, Harry answered: "You will remain a Coast Guard Officer, with existing rank and all service advancement opportunities, and that does not matter to us; we often have multiple services working together." Then with a smile, added: "And, as I've often reminded Admiral Wicks, in Wartime, the Coast Guard falls under the Navy's jurisdiction anyway."

Then with a very serious tone to his voice, said: "We do not take your decision lightly, again I say that it is yours alone, and we have full respect and regard for whatever you decide.

CHAPTER SIX

Tuesday, 26 March 2019
United States Naval Weapons Station
Yorktown, Virginia

Commander Harold Jarrett drove down to Yorktown early Tuesday morning to see if he could find someone who could tell him something about the weapon systems on a Russian submarine. Specifically, he wanted to know as clear as possible, was there any way the explosion on the Nikolayevich Kosinski could have been an accident.

He, Paul, and Linda had spent all afternoon yesterday trying to see what this incident could be all about. They looked at what occurred, the response of the Russian Captain, and the crew's response. Was there a reason for it to be planned, and many other points that might bring them an answer?

They tried to apply various reasons for its destruction to have been of any value to the Russians, only to come back to the basic fact that Russia had lost a half a billion-dollar nuclear submarine; so, why?

After several hours of discussion, it was Linda who finely said: "Gentlemen, I am not in the Navy, but I was a state trooper investigator, and one of the things I learned, early in my tenure, was don't try to create a crime if there was any chance at all that it could have been an accident.

"So, before we tear our brains out, let us find out as sure as possible that there was no chance that it wasn't simply an accident."

It was that statement from Linda that had Harold on the road to Yorktown early Tuesday morning.

After arriving at the weapons headquarters building, he was shown into a conference room where three people waited for him. Lieutenant Commander John Watts, Lieutenant Phil Caswell, and Chief Petty Officer Stephen Marks greeted him with reserved interest.

Harold said: "Thank you for your response to our request for knowledge regarding the radioactive leak aboard the Russian submarine, the Nikolayevich Kosinski.

"We at NSIU have been tasked to find a possible reason for the incident, including the possible exclusion of it being accidental.

"Responding to our initial request from DOD and the AEC, as well as our nuclear fleet in New London, they all indicated an explosion near the reactor cover would be necessary for such a loss of containment. Their feelings are that it is highly unlikely, based upon the presumed fact that there should never be explosives anywhere near a reactor."

Lieutenant Caswell said: "I can verify that we in our nuclear vessels never allow any explosives within the same compartment where any part of a reactor has any exposure. I can't answer for the Russians, but they follow the same procedure from all we know."

Lieutenant Commander Watts indicated: "Part of the reason for that, any reactor bay is lined with a lead sheathing in case of a radioactive leak." Turning towards Chief Marks, he said: "You have been fortunate enough to get aboard a Russian Nuclear Sub Chief, are we stating the correct information?"

Sitting at the table with his hands crossed, Chief Marks said: "Yes Sir, but it goes much further than that. You see, the reactor bay is usually 'aft' (back) from the rear end of the sail (the topside tower). It is located there for access to provide special service and for fueling. But Russian subs have a much longer sail than we do on our boats. So, the reactor bay is located quite farther back from amidships.

"What makes it all unlikely accidental is that their weapons are all in compartments, not anywhere close!"

"I see," said Harold: "I presume that you also feel that an accident is unlikely."

"Yes, Sir," said Chief Marks, "but there is another reason.

"You see, there were no real casualties, only minor exposures, and although there are several crew members located to the rear of the reactor bay, the ship's Captain had to have sufficient control to surface.

"Then, upon surfacing, he needed to seal off the 'aft' part of the boat. However, someone had to have access to the manual propulsion controls during these actions, and they are located further 'aft' the reactor bay.

"The duration of radioactive exposure was very short before the entire crew was above decks waiting to be rescued. That would only take a few minutes."

"Lieutenant Commander Watts said: "As Chief Marks indicated, it all happened very quickly, and our ships were very close by and able to affect a rescue in short order. The Russians would likely have known that such quick attention would occur."

Harold looked at Chief Marks, then realizing what he had said, understood that any possibility of it being accidental was all but eliminated.

Expressing his appreciation for the information that they had provided, Harold left and headed back to Washington. It would be too late in the day to go back to his office, so he headed home and sat at his laptop and entered notes of the opinions he had obtained.

Early Wednesday morning, as he walked into the building on his way to his office, the Admiral called out to him as he passed the door. Turning around and entering the Admiral's office, he was told that he might expect a call from a Lieutenant Commander Connie Wall from the Coast Guard.

Then the Admiral told him about his impromptu visit to New London yesterday, and his opinion of the young woman he had met. He also handed him a copy of her military file that he had received from Admiral Wicks.

He said: "I think we may have hit a home run here, but please form your own opinion, and you may assure her that we in the Navy understand and appreciate that she is a Coast Guard officer."

Harold then proceeded up to the break room and was pouring a coffee, when both Paul and Linda walked in together.

Linda said: "Good morning, how was your trip down to Yorktown yesterday?"

Harold responded: "Good morning," and handing her a copy of the notes he prepared the previous evening, said: "I think we have a crime! The only trouble is we have no idea exactly what the crime is!"

Linda started to read through his notes and then passed them over to Paul as he sat down and placed a cup of coffee in front of her.

"I see your point," he said after reading through them, "but where do we go from here?"

It was Linda who answered that question: "Well, I believe that before we go anywhere with this, we need to find out who would benefit from such an action."

Harold said: "I agree, but about the only thing unlikely is that it would be the current Russian government to be the one. However, the question comes to mind; is there a problem that we don't know about within that government?"

Paul answered: "None that I've heard, but maybe that is a question we need to ask the State Department."

Linda responded: "There are frequent reports about the Russian president and his absolute control over their Politburo, can there be a possible Coup d'état forming?"

Paul said: "They largely run a secret government, but maybe someone is trying to make a change."

Harold responded: "True, but let's not look only there; is it possible for some other foreign influence to be involved? Perhaps as retribution for an action that had been taken against them?"

Paul stood up and started to pace around the room. Stopping, he turned and said: "All this is simply speculation. The fact is the Russians lost a valuable submarine and were embarrassed on the world stage. The only ones who could tell us about it are the Russian crew of that Sub, and they will never be available for us to ask."

Linda said: "Did anyone look at the report from the Coast Guard ship that was first to respond? I don't know their policy, but I presume they would follow normal procedures, and that includes recording the names and personal addresses of all those people rescued."

With a smile on his face, Paul said: "Linda, once again, you come up with a possible path for us to follow. I never thought of that, but of course, we would have their names, ranks, service numbers, and yes, even possibly their addresses.

"With the obvious extent of a radioactive leak and the ultimate scuttling of the Sub in deep water by a joint effort of our Navy and the Russian Navy, all the news and reports would be about the issues of containing and securing safe disposal of the problem. Then the embarrassment of the Russians and the cooperative effort from our people to secure safe results would push that detail into a back pocket."

Harold responded: "You may be right, Paul, let me put a call into State and see if they have heard anything, then I'll check with DOD and see if there is a copy of the Coast Guard rescue report we can look at."

CHAPTER SEVEN

Friday, 29 March 2019
NSIU Headquarters
Washington D.C.

This week the people at NSIU had accustomed themselves to several changes in their operations and procedures. Some were expected, and some were new. For the first time, in several years, Jane McCalla wasn't there.

Most of the seal team had just returned from doing cold weather refresher activities in Kodiak, Alaska, and Chief Ira Jones was home from a long two-week vacation in Western Canada.

So, when the Friday morning meeting took place at ten o'clock, there would be much new information to sort out.

The third-floor conference room was full. Everyone was sitting and chatting about the recent events when the Admiral entered, followed by Coast Guard Lieutenant Commander Connie Wall, and Commander Harold Jarrett.

As the room became quiet, the Admiral said, "I want you all to meet Lieutenant Commander Connie Wall, who has graciously agreed to join our unit." Then motioning clockwise around the table, proceeded to introduced everyone present by name.

Then he said: "Some of you might have missed it, but Lieutenant Jane McCalla has moved over to the State Department and is now their official spokesperson. It is a wonderful opportunity for her, and we all wish her the very best. However, it left us short a very important part of our group.

When I reached out, looking for someone to help us coordinate our investigating operations, we were extremely lucky to find the Lieutenant Commander. With a little encouragement, she was willing to make a huge change from being a Coast Guard OCS instructor in New London, Connecticut, to applying her talents and help with our operations here in Washington.

Then turning to her, said, as he motioned towards them: "Connie, these eight very peaceful looking gentlemen, sitting here are all experienced U.S. Navy Seals, and you may rest assured, they usually know how to get the job done. "Then, gesturing towards Linda, said: "Linda, as a civilian contract investigator, is a former Vermont State Police Sergeant who came to us after we had a very difficult coordinated case that first appeared in her home state.

Continuing, he said: "Lonnie has been with us for a long time, and he is also a civilian contract employee. He handles all of our necessary paperwork, along with our two very special Navy yeomen; Jimmy Louis and Susan Gordon. As a lawyer, any legal situations or questions that somehow always seem to occur are handled within his province.

Taking a slow glance around the room, he continued: "I think that everyone here, along with you, Harold, and me, all in the same room, at the same time, is indeed a rare occurrence. So, let us make use of it and find out what we all have been doing and where we think we might need to go."

As the Admiral, Harold and Connie sat down, Linda said: "I am pleased to meet you, Lieutenant Commander, and look forward to spending some time with you as we move through some of the most confusing projects that just seem to find their way before us."

At that moment, Harold spoke up: "Before we get too far into various projects, I had a chance to spend some time yesterday with Connie, and explained that we are indeed a diverse group of military officers, enlisted personnel, and civilians. With that said, I explained that for the most part, we put all formal exchanges aside whenever we can, and use a first name basis with each other."

Connie spoke up with a smile and said: "I thank the Admiral and Harold for their kind words, and I would be pleased and honored to have you all call me Connie."

Then with a short chuckle, she said: "Forgive me for laughing a little bit, but as you have just heard, I come from an instructor's position at the Coast Guard Officers Candidate School; everything there is precisely opposite from this and very formal. I believe I am going to enjoy this relaxed atmosphere so much better."

For the next two hours, the general discussion encompassed a recount of all the team's events for the past few weeks.

Ira had been on a helicopter skiing vacation up in the Canadian Rockies. Except for Paul, the other seals had all been in Kodiak, Alaska, doing a special cold weather isolation refresher course.

Paul and Linda, along with Harold, explained their current investigation about the Russian Sub incident.

Harold passed out copies of his beginning notes showing what was in the news, what had been described by the State Department briefing, and from his trip down to the Yorktown weapons center.

As everyone read over his notes, he said: "I think you will see that we believe the incident was most assuredly not an accident. If that is the case, then it was deliberate, and the question is, why?"

Paul added: "We do believe it was deliberate, and to add to Harold's question, I think we need to find out who would benefit from such an extreme action?

"We are only at the beginning of this investigation, but I think we may be involved with something that could be very sinister. Please don't hesitate to put forward any ideas or suggestions, no matter how insignificant they may seem at the time."

With a big smile on her face, Linda said: "Connie, please don't get the wrong idea, but having you here, at this particular time, is simply amazing.

"Harold, Paul, and I have been discussing this for several days. As you can see in Harold's notes, the description of the incident stated that the first vessels on the scene were a couple of American commercial fishing boats and a U. S. Coast Guard Cutter; a short time later, they were joined by several U. S. Navy ships.

"My question to you, as a Coast Guard Officer, is about official maritime rescue procedure.

"We, in the Vermont state police, and all other first responders that I know of, record the names and as much available information from the individuals they rescue as possible.

"Is that procedure the same in an incident such as this?

"It was the fisherman who helped transport most of the crew from the stricken Submarine to the Coast Guard Cutter, and the Sub's crew members then remained aboard, and were treated, until they were transferred to a Russian support ship several hours later.

"My question, therefore, is, would the Coast Guard have a list of all the Russian crew members, their names, ranks, service numbers, and maybe even home addresses? And, if so, where would that information be kept?"

Connie glanced at Linda with a strange look in her eye and said: "Coast Guard Rescue procedures are the same. When the military is directly involved, those records become a permanent part of the ship's log. That is true in both commercial maritime vessels and the Coast Guard as well."

Linda asked: "Does anyone look at them or usually request them?"

Connie said: "Not unless specifically asked, or if a medical notification is involved. Of course, the official report is a detailed summary of the event; but that personal degree of detail, although available, is usually not included."

The Admiral asked Linda: "Do you think that specific detail is going to be needed?"

Harold, answering for her, said: "Well yes, Sir, we are looking at it as probably a sabotage case because we don't believe it was an accident; therefore, who might have had a reason to do it?"

CHAPTER EIGHT

Sunday, 31 March 2019
Hotel Lake Luzern
Rue du Lausanne
Lausanne, Switzerland

British entrepreneur Christopher Bing, sipping a cappuccino, sat waiting at one of his Hotel's outside porch tables. On this cool day in Lausanne, he was waiting for the meeting he had scheduled with Darvish Abthai, the local attaché from Iran to Switzerland.

Bing had received a communication from a reliable contact he had in Russia, Boris Kanski, suggesting that he might be wise to listen to Abthai's comments and recommendations.

Bing is the CEO of a British North Sea offshore drilling company. His Company, 'Deep Ice Oil,' competes with many international organizations, including many Russian, Arab, and even Iranian companies, for those very lucrative European Union contracts that are known to purchase large quantities of crude oil.

Changes in the drilling and refining of crude oil, both technological and political, have occurred during the past few years. Those changes have made the United States, previously a major importer; now, one of the largest producers of both finished and crude oil products globally, making them almost totally self-sufficient.

That competitive edge, going to the United States, has allowed for unusual alliances between many other oil-producing countries, creating cooperation and agreements where they had never been before.

Many Arab countries had supplied much of the world's fuel energy needs for some time. However, various wars, political actions, and even religious differences, that had been in place for years, were failing; with the resulting costs skyrocketing. Throughout most oil-producing countries, that, and reasonable production practices, had created a major shift in source availability.

However, the need was still there, and those Arab countries responded to the economic changes as well; yet the supply chain had shifted. Countries that had been a reliable source of exported oil found themselves in a far more competitive market than ever before.

With America increasing their availability to supply oil, it was no longer needed for them to import crude from those foreign sources. That created a shift of supply to the remaining parts of the industrial world, and they were now far more competitive than ever before. The competition was the driver to lower costs; thus, many Arab suppliers felt their economies shrink for the first time in years.

Bing had been sitting and waiting for Abthai for about twenty minutes when the overweight Iranian strode in and sat down.

"It has been a while since we've seen each other," said Abthai. "How are you doing in the cold North Sea?"

Having met Abthai over a year ago at an economic show in Belgium, Bing responded with no change of expression, "I am fine! I understand you have some recommendations that might interest me."

Abthai, clasping his hands together, said: "The Americans are causing a change in our economy. They are no longer the world's consumer of crude oil, and we have felt the loss in profit to be significant. I am sure that you, too, have felt it."

Bing stared at him but said nothing.

"Well," continued Abthai, "we think that we need to do something to level the field and find a new way of cutting their impact on the world's market.

"Boris Kanski told me that you are also suffering profit decline and are moving to lower production costs. Is that correct?"

Bing, not very comfortable with this Iranian, sighed and said: "Yes, we have seen a loss in profit, and that is why we are pushing for more of the European Union contracts; however, it is the Russians and you Iranians who are our primary competitors."

Abthai said: "Perhaps that could be altered, and we might be able to push the Russians out of that particular market. Would that be of interest to you?"

Bing looked into the eyes of Abthai and slowly answered: "Just what are you implying? Do you have some control over the Russians?"

Abthai sat back and, with a sly smile, said: "Perhaps! Do you remember that Russian nuclear submarine incident off the Aleutian Islands in the United States territory about three months ago?"

Bing nodded: "The one with the radioactive leakage that forced it's scuddling in deep water?

"What about it?"

Abthai said: "What if I told you that we knew about that accident almost six months ago and that we can probably foresee additional embarrassments between the Russians and the Americans?"

Bing just looked at him for several minutes, then said: "Why are you telling me this fairytale? Are you saying that you are capable of controlling what the Russians may do?"

"Perhaps," Abthai said: "I have known Boris for many years, and we both have many mutual connections."

Bing said: "Again, I ask, why are you telling me this?"

Abthai answered: "If we have access to your source of crude available, and along with ours, we possibly could create a situation for a major withdrawal of Russian crude supplies to the EU!

"If that happens, the Americans will end up shouldering the blame. Relations between the two countries are never on solid ground, so with another similar instance where the Russians suffer another embarrassment at the Americans' hands, we could move ahead of them with control of the oil distribution in eastern and western Europe.

Bing, shaking his head, said: "How do you want me to answer this? I have only your word that you can control the Russians, and that is indeed a stretch."

Abthai raised his eyebrows at that statement, and said: "Perhaps I have misjudged your desire to obtain a larger share of the European market?"

Bing just looked at him, and again said nothing.

Abthai said: "We are, by no means, friends with the Americans, but it is the Russians who now are in our economic way, and we have had to access certain resources that have been below the radar there for many years.

"However, if we can close down the availability of a large part of the Russian European supply chain, they would be forced to try and compete for some of the control the Americans have taken from the world's market. And that would allow us better access to the EU."

CHAPTER NINE

Monday, 1 April 2019
NSIU Headquarters
Washington D.C.

The weekend for Connie had been busy. She had flown back to New London Friday afternoon and was closing up her apartment to move out.

Realizing that, although she hadn't accumulated a lot of things over the last seven years, there were at least twice as many items as she thought she had.

With an amicable agreement from her landlord, she was able to extend her move out date for a few days; and arranged for her stuff to be picked up and delivered to a storage shed in Washington, where her furniture and things could be stored.

She didn't know exactly where she would move to yet, but Admiral Walker had arranged temporary housing for her at a nearby bed and breakfast.

Surprisingly, the Coast Guard and the Navy worked well together to arrange for her transfer from Connecticut to Washington with little delay.

As she walked into NSIU at nine o'clock Monday morning, she was greeted by Linda, who had just arrived at the same time.

"Good morning Connie," she said pleasantly; "how did you make out this weekend with your transfer?"

Connie, getting used to the informal ways of NSIU and enjoying the friendly atmosphere answered: "Good morning Linda, I haven't moved much in the past seven years, and I am finding that it is more of a challenge than I thought.

"However, everyone has been so pleasant and helpful that I am learning a whole new way of getting things done."

"It will get easier," said Linda; "When I came down from Vermont, awhile back, I also found that the people here are truly dedicated to the task at hand, and jointly always work closely together.

"If you need a little help or guidance finding a place, any of us would be glad to help you get settled."

As they walked to the break room for coffee, they found Paul and Luigi already there reading through the morning's reports.

Luigi and Paul both stood up, and Luigi said: "Good morning ladies. Then looking over at Connie, continued, "Connie, did you get the things done this weekend you needed to?"

Connie relaxed and said: "It has just begun. Funny, I don't remember getting all the stuff I seem to have accumulated, so I needed to rent a larger storage shed than I thought, but hopefully, it won't be long before I find a new place."

Paul said: "If you like, we all would be glad to help you find your way around, and don't hesitate to ask.

"I checked with Harold this morning, and your new office is on the second floor just down the hall from the elevator. When you finish your coffee, we can take you there and help you get settled."

Luigi than said: "The schedule, this morning, is for a general assignment meeting in the conference room at ten o'clock. Since most of us have been away for a few weeks, it should be interesting to see what mischief has reared its ugly head while we were gone."

At the ten o'clock general meeting, the conference room was again filled near to capacity. Friendly chatter, in the room, was about things everyone had been doing during the past few weeks. And that included Connie's welcomed addition to the team.

When the Admiral and Harold entered and sat down, the chatter subsided.

"Good morning," said the Admiral. "Before we get started, I want to say that it is good to see you all back and ready to go.

"I got a call from Jane this morning, and she said that although she misses everyone, her new challenge is fascinating, and probably is going to give her gray hair at an early age."

Turning to Connie, he added: "I told her of you joining our unit, and she was so pleased that you could become available right away. I agree with her about that."

Harold picking up several files said: "On to things at hand; first, we have many items here, in this morning's correspondence:

"Item number one. Paul, your favorite topic, rears up again in Chicago. Over the weekend, there were two riots and eleven gang-related shootings that took place. Fortunately, there were no deaths this time, but again several abusive political statements, reported in the news, sent this back to the DOD, and thus on to us."

Paul answered: "I feel like a broken record; this is a local problem; what do they expect from us?"

"Who knows," responded Harold, "but please send a note to DOD about it.

"Item number two," he continued: "There was an explosion in Sharjah, over in the United Arab Emirates (UAE). Several large oil storage tanks exploded on the peninsula, east of the Khalid Lagoon, by the docks' loading pier. DOD thinks that it is very questionable. The Arabs aren't sure that it wasn't possibly an accident, but they also feel it might have been targeted. However, how and by whom?

"Ira, would you please look into this? Maybe you will need a team, but let's find out whatever we can before going over there."

Ira said: "I actually agree with DOD. Those storage tanks are right on the Strait of Hormuz, just a short distance across the Persian Gulf to Iran."

"Continuing onto item number three," said Harold: "There seems to be some trouble again in Tehran. There was a riot again last night, and it is the local people still trying to gain some control over their government. Probably not much we should do, but would you look into the details Rudy and write a report?

"Also, check with the State Department to see if they have any specific directive we should follow."

"Will do!" said Rudy as he added the notes to his notebook.

"Item number four," said Harold: "DOD asks for any further information regarding the Russian sub incident. They seem to be watching it closely, and they haven't heard anything new from the Russians.

"Paul, will you, Linda, and maybe you too Luigi, focus on this; we think that there is much more to learn than we've seen so far.

"Also, we've pretty much agreed, amongst ourselves, that it wasn't an accident. With that thought in mind, let us look into three major areas of concern: One, who did it, two, what is gained from the loss, and three, why are we involved?"

The Admiral spoke up for the first time, saying: "I think, since the parties involved include actions from the Coast Guard, and we now have Connie with us, it seems that she would be a good addition to that team as well.

"Also, as Harold just said, DOD is a bit nervous about the potential actions that could result from this incident, and so is the State Department."

"Item number five," Harold continued: "DOD is concerned that Venezuela's situation is on the verge of another public uprising again. There may be another food shortage showing there and a health crisis that could cross over into Colombia.

"That leaves Antonio, David, John, and Peter available to look into that.

"Antonio, please check with State and see if there is anything they may know about the rumor. Also, I suggest that, for now, you all help Ira find the cause of the explosions, in the Emirates; and yet be available to work with Paul, Linda, Luigi, and Connie on the Russian Sub incident."

Turning towards the Admiral, Harold said: "I believe, sir, that is all in the DOD report."

The Admiral said: "This looks like it could turn into a busy week, so let's figure on an afternoon update meeting each day beginning tomorrow; if everyone now knows what to do, this meeting is adjourned."

CHAPTER TEN

Monday, 1 April 2019
Russian Naval Secretary's Office
Moscow, Russia

Victor Polanski, the Russian head of naval operations, had returned to Moscow from Vladivostok three weeks ago. He was still severely puzzled by the Nikolayevich Kosinski's loss in the Bering Sea.

The embarrassment that Russia had suffered had settled down, but it would always be there, just below the surface in various political discussions.

The main problem that he was still facing is what had caused the radioactive leak. Even though he had conducted extensive interviews and held a strong control over the ship captain's future, he hadn't been able to discover anything that would point to an understandable reason.

The thirty-six-man crew, of mostly officers, had all survived. And although eight of them suffered a significant amount of radioactive poisoning, none were life-threatening.

The results from the crew member's interviews failed to reveal anything more than a statement that some type, or sort, of explosion occurred in the primary reactor bay. But there was no explanation of what had caused it.

Pressure from the Defense Director and several Politburo members to determine an acceptable reason for Russia's political embarrassment did little to help find a solution. However, that pressure was beginning to take a toll on Polanski, and he knew he had little time left to come up with a logical explanation and perhaps point blame at some of the crew and the captain.

The Nikolayevich Kosinski had been officially on an assigned mission to intercept and monitor American communications.

However, he had privately been told that they were supposedly there to determine if the Americans were proceeding to build another loading port station, which several of their supertankers could use. If so, that would allow for an increase in crude oil from the Alaska fields.

Although the Alaska Pipe Line had been in use for several decades, the Americans continued to increase their lead in oil production and move it away from what had been previously foreign-sourced.

The loss of Mid-Eastern crude oil export into the United States had changed the dynamic of fossil fuel energy supplies throughout Europe and the Middle East. Ultimately it forced Russia to be in an uncomfortable competitive position with the Middle East suppliers for those areas not previously contested.

These were the official reasons that had been given to Victor Polanski and the Russian Navy.

However, the real reason the Sub was there was because the Defense Director and those few Politburo officials had secretly rigged a different assignment situation.

They were trying to find a way to recreate a similar disaster to that of the 1989 Exxon Valdez oil spill. A similar situation would cause a significant environmental and political reaction, and at the same time, cause an embarrassing international situation for the United States.

Those officials secretly ordered the Sub's Captain to have them sail close to the American coastline. The Americans would know it was there, of course, and assume they were only on a surveillance mission.

Its close in position to the shore, would allow a special remote underwater sabotage team to secretly offload twenty explosively charged barrels of oil and anchor them to the sea bottom in shallow water. It was set to create an unidentifiable oil spill in the same general area where the Exxon Valdez had ruptured thirty years ago.

It was planned that after the Sub had arranged for the placement of almost eleven-hundred gallons of crude oil, it would be far away before they remotely triggered the leak. The resulting spill would have a serious effect on the ocean surface, creating an embarrassing containment situation for the Americans.

This plan had been formed by several senior Politburo members and instigated without the Russian head of naval operations input. They thought that the resulting outcry from international conservationists, anti-energy pundits, and the political action groups would cause such an embarrassment to the Americans that it could likely force a change in the supply chain, maybe even back to the previous way.

The failure in the reactor bay and the ultimate result, however, changed all that! The resulting embarrassment was for the Russians, not the Americans.

There were going to be some changes in the planning and authorization of future missions, including several high party officials probably disappearing, with new permanent Siberian assignments.

Victor Polanski did not want to be one of them!

CHAPTER ELEVEN

Over the past few days, things were, for the most part, normal. However, several investigation projects had found a new life, and, not surprisingly, there was only a little change in some of the others.

Ira had been following reports about the fuel tank explosion incident in Sharjah, and their local investigation. Now, however, the UAE had asked for some input and investigation help from the United States.

The UAE is made up of separate states, and each is independent from the others. But they can, and upon occasion will, act together if one is threatened; also, they share a national court system.

In Sharjah, the local preliminary investigation resulted in more questions than answers. Although no record was found that showed any sinister behavior when the fuel tanks exploded, their initial review showed that it didn't seem like the cause was within the site's confines.

Recent events had resulted in a healthy relationship with the United States, so when their local people asked for someone to help determine the cause of the explosion, the State Department responded with a representative, and several DOD explosive expert investigators. DOD also asked NSIU to send a small security team to accompany the technical team.

With the unknown cause of an explosion and its proximity to Iran, only about 220 km (135 mi) across the sea, DOD felt that a small knowledgeable seal team would be an asset to the investigation. That request resulted in Ira, Antonio, David, and Peter joining with a DOS representative and two Army technical experts.

The complete USA team, left Washington to fly over to Dubai yesterday afternoon. Together with Sharjah's experts, they would try to determine what had happened.

Moving to the Tehran incidents, Rudy spent time over at both DOD and the State Department, learning all the latest information. He was trying to determine what, if anything, was needed to understand the cause of the riots. He was able to meet Jane at her new office, and together, along with a State Department advisor, they met with, and talked to, the local Swiss Attaché to the USA, and learned how the uprising had been handled.

The only determination they could find was the general population was not happy with the current Islamic Republic leadership, and was looking for a change.

They learned that the Swiss had closed their embassy in Tehran so as not to allow sanctuary for the protesters; this was the second time in just a month. The Swiss policy of having an uninvolved approach to the Iranian problem was still intact. This policy had the added positive effect of keeping the rest of the world aware of what was going on.

Back at NSIU, Paul, Linda, Connie, and Luigi moved along with research about the Russian Sub incident.

Upon request to the Joint Alaska Command, they had been able to obtain our country's tracking record of the Nikolayevich Kosinski's spying route; and the report of the extensive joint American and Russian effort needed to handle its safe disposal after the incident.

After studying the American tracking chart, that the Russian Submarine had been following, Connie just sat quietly with a frown on her face. Luigi, who had been watching her for a while, realized that something she read was disturbing her.

He said: "I presume, Connie, you see something that we didn't and wonder why none of us picked up on it."

Connie looked up at Luigi, smiled and answered: "No, it isn't that at all; I am just wondering why a Russian, Akula-class submarine, at almost six-hundred feet in length and seventy-five feet wide, would track within two to two-and-a-half miles off our coastline, particularly when there are so much safer waters just four miles further out.

"The tracking report says it was that close, following the shoreline's curves the entire time."

Paul looked up at that and said: "I believe you have a point. They surely would know that we were tracking their every move, and communications monitoring doesn't need to be anywhere near that close."

Luigi said: "Do you think they had some other intention? If so, what?"

"I don't know," said Connie, "but those are relatively shallow waters for such a large sub, yet they stayed close in and submerged, all along the outer chain of the Aleutian Islands.

"I can assure you that any vessel near those dimensions, either surface or submersible, would be very uncomfortable in those waters. Also, surface currents are frequently severe and very often unpredictable."

Paul said: "Why would they stay so close in, near those islands? They are mostly volcanic and, for the most part, completely uninhabited.

"Atka Island, where they finally surfaced, is itself, really nothing more than a wildlife preserve, and that is where they surfaced after the explosion."

Linda, who had been quietly sitting listening, said: "Interesting points, but the facts are there before us. I do have one question though, did any of our monitoring pick up the actual time of the alleged explosion aboard the Sub?"

All three of the others turned to Linda and just stared.

Paul finely asked the question they all had: "Why do you ask that?"

With a slight smile on her face, Linda said: "Well, we all have said several times that we believe the explosion was not an accident. So, I wonder, did it occur before or after the Sub surfaced? If before, Harold's information, that he learned in Yorktown, would suggest that there would be a lot more casualties than there were. If after it surfaced, then the Captain and probably several of his crew planned it."

"We all agree with that," said Paul, "but that just puts us back in the corner where there seems to be no explanation."

Linda, turning to Connie, said: "Connie, when you first came here last week, I asked you if the crew names would be in the official report, do you remember?"

Connie answered with raised eyebrows: "Yes, and I told you that they would have been recorded and kept in the rescue ship's log."

Linda said: "Do you know how we could get a copy of that log with those names and information?"

Quietly, Connie turned to pick up the overall report and looked through it. After about a minute, she looked up and said: "Here it is, and it is a big one, about three-hundred and eighty feet, a High Endurance Coast Guard Cutter named the 'Charles of Alaska.' It is stationed at the Joint Base Elmendorf-Richardson, Alaska Command.

"A ship's log is special and usually very protected. Command will want to know why we want it, and I think we need to explain that we are in an active investigation under direction from the DOD, and an official request, signed by the Admiral, will be necessary.

"The Submarine crew was, most likely, all Russian, so why the question?"

Linda said: "I learned a few years ago that the assumption of what appears to be an obvious fact sometimes, we find, isn't a fact at all. So, the question is, who on that crew has reason enough to risk it all?

"By learning all we can get about each crew member as an individual person, and not just as a Russian sailor, we might find there may be a reason along with a strong enough incentive for him to take such an action."

Luigi had been quiet through most of the discussion, but something was pulling at him that just wouldn't go away. His thoughts were along the line of why was the Submarine even there in the first place? The reasons advanced that it was on a spying mission to monitor communications and make what coastal observations they could; just rang hollow to him.

There were many ways to monitor communications; some were by radio interception, some through satellite monitoring, and extremely accurate shoreline photographs could determine the coastline within inches. The Russians would assuredly know that the Sub's route was not needed for any survey, so why was it following such a course?

CHAPTER TWELVE

Thursday, 4 April 2019
Container Shipping and Fuel Storage Facility
Sharjah, United Arab Emirates

As the American representatives, and explosive experts, arrived at the Dubai International airport early Thursday morning, they were met by the local ministry representatives from Sharjah. Four special vehicles were waiting for the Americans, and they were quickly cleared and left for the Copthorne Hotel in Sharjah, where they would be staying.

After checking in, they were taken over to the seaport to see where the tanks had exploded and given a quick tour of the damaged area.

There were several areas where various tanks are, but the six tanks located next to each other had suffered the damage from the explosion.

Local UAE experts had found that the tops on two of the tanks had partially lifted off due to the fuel igniting the explosion inside. But on a third tank, the top had been sucked in as the tank actually imploded. All of the tanks contained similar fuels, so why did two explode and only one implode?

The site's damage was extensive, and both the American experts, along with the UAE experts, began to look at each area with meticulous care.

The NSIU team also began to study the event, looking for anything that would indicate that there might have been a possible infiltration, or unauthorized access, aimed at a potential sabotage effort. The UAE experts, also looking at that possibility, provided a record of people who had access and had been on-site over the last ninety days. The only thing that had been eliminated was that no external bomb was remotely fired at the site from any known location or force.

Although the UAE had grown over the past few decades, from an Arab tribal chieftain society into a wealthy international culture, they were still very reliant on the export of crude oil for almost half of their economic income. So, with this explosion, there was much concern as to the cause.

On the western and southern shores of the Persian Gulf, this area of the Middle East had been part of the world's premier supplier of crude oil for decades. But changes in the world's supply chain can cause competition amongst the various suppliers where it hadn't previously existed.

The basic fact that Iran was on the eastern shore of the Persian Gulf and occasionally took action against its western neighbors for their trade with Europe and America could be a problem. The NSIU team had that thought in their heads from the very beginning of the investigation.

Ira, David, Peter, and Antonio took the records that they were provided, and along with the UAE local investigators, as a group, studied the information available about the people who have had site access.

This seaport is a very busy place with cargo containers, fuel storage tanks, loading, or unloading container ships tied to the piers. Even helicopter landing vessels are kept there for access to remote areas and islands. As a result, the list of people with access was sizeable, several hundred over those ninety days.

The task at hand was difficult, for most people had good reason to be where they were. However, amongst the two investigation teams, they were able to reduce the people of interest down to about a dozen.

It was at this point that the two different cultures between the Americans and the UAE became interesting. Of the dozen people they had isolated from the list, all were men, none were from the UAE, all had been alone while on-site, and little was known for the reason they were there. However, the local investigators tended to believe that since they were all young men, and although not from the UAE, they probably were just visiting from their Arab neighbors to learn about shipping procedures. The NSIU was not so sure.

By the end of Thursday afternoon, there was still no finite proof of the explosion's cause, so they all retired for the day and figured to start again tomorrow morning.

The NSIA team, along with the joint UAE and American explosive experts, had been busy all weekend looking into the possibility that the two fuel tank explosions and the third fuel tank's collapse were an accident caused by carelessness.

The attendant, who was in charge of loading fuel to the small tanker, said that it was a standard procedure to check that the vent line valve was open; before any fuel transfer was begun, he was positive that he had done so. Yet, when the damaged tank was inspected, they found the vent valve had been closed.

However, that didn't explain the other two tanks exploding, and the damage to those was severe.

The American explosive experts were sure that the cause of those tank explosions was from an external source. But the tank tops had blown out, and that was a sure sign of an internal blast. So how had they ignited?

There are only two pipes connected to a tank, one is to fill it with fuel or pump the fuel out, and the other pipe is the vent pipe to allow air into or out of the tank during pumping operations.

When Ira asked if they could review the security camera recordings, he and several UAE investigators went over to a small conference room.

Over the next three hours, together they reviewed all of the area recordings; everything seemed normal.

It was a boring and tedious process, but for some reason, both Ira and Casper, one of the Sharjah investigators, would not look away from the TV screen; even for a moment. They both saw it at the same time.

A tall thin man, dressed in a traditional white thobe and wearing a white kaffiyeh strolled back and forth past the tanks three separate times.

When the operator left the tanks and drove away in his truck, to make sure the ship's transfer was going all right, the thin man quickly leaned over and quite clearly closed the vent valve. Then looking all around, he leaned over the pipes by the other two tanks' vent lines and did something to each of them that they couldn't see. He then immediately turned and headed towards the exit gates.

He was too far away to get a good look at his face. But as he walked behind some freight containers, he disappeared for a moment, only to again appear on the other side of them, as he continued walking towards the gate guard. But his kaffiyeh was now plaid.

They now knew that it wasn't an accident and knew that it was done by an individual who wanted not to be identified. Casper turned, looked at Ira, and said: "We have made a terrible mistake. We assumed that none of our visitors that day could have been involved. Clearly, one of them was. If you forgive me for our blindness, I'd like to help you determine which visitor it was.

Ira, always the diplomat whenever he was speaking to a foreign fellow investigator, said: "We saw it together, and we need your special knowledge to see if we can determine who that man is."

Casper, able to regain some of his lost pride, said: "I believe we may already know who he is. The kaffiyeh he is wearing, as he left, is the plaid of Yemen."

Then looking at the visitor list, he said: "There was only one visitor that day from Yemen, his name is Ahmad Abd-El-Kader, and he is from Sana'a."

CHAPTER THIRTEEN

Friday, 5 April 2019
NSIU Headquarters
Washington D.C.

L uigi was still unusually quiet when the team met Friday morning. He thought about the Russian Submarine's path and was trying to develop an acceptable reason for their strange route.

The general theory, being passed around, assumed that it was on a typical espionage mission, and, although supposedly secret, it was well known and accepted by the United States authorities. The assumption reasoned that somehow it got too close to the shoreline and was caught off-guard when an explosion ruptured the reactor bay.

But Luigi kept hearing, in his head, Connie's comment about dangerous waters so near to the shore; that, and the fact that it just wasn't necessary for them to be that close for any such a mission. So why were they there, and what was their plan?

Connie had prepared an official request, to be signed by the admiral, then sent, through DOD, to the Coast Guard Joint Base Elmendorf-Richardson, Alaska Command. It requested a photocopy be made of the ship's log about the incident, including collecting the Russian sailors' names and personal information, while they were being treated, aboard the 'Charles of Alaska. It was requested that it be faxed to the NSIU for the DOD investigation as soon as possible.

Harold, Connie, Linda, and Paul's conversations were general, and not much was said other than they would have to wait for the Coast Guard log report.

Finally, Luigi spoke up: "We don't know, but can we look at possible reasons for that Sub to have been there in the first place?

"I, for one, am having a hard time believing that the Captain, or for that matter, his entire crew would venture into those waters on a simple espionage mission. It just doesn't make sense. As Connie said yesterday, those are known treacherous waters with unpredictable currents. Does anyone believe that the Russian Captain wouldn't have known that?

"So, for what other reason could he have been there, where had he come from, where was he headed, and most importantly, what were his intentions?"

Harold looked over at Luigi and said: "You have a look in your eye, what makes you think we are maybe on the wrong track?"

Luigi looked back at Harold and replied: "Well, he was on the north side of the island chain, albeit still pretty far west on the chain. It has been stated that he was following the physical coastline just two to two-and-a-half miles offshore.

"We all know that the topography for that area is that of a deep ocean mountain range, just below the surface. Those islands that are above the surface are, for the most part, developed volcanoes, some dormant, and some still active. At least at the remote area where the incident occurred.

"So, I ask, why was he on the north side in the Bearing sea, as opposed to calmer and deeper waters of the North Pacific, on the south side, just a few miles away?"

Connie, sitting back in her chair, said: "You have a point, Luigi, it is even reasonably easy to find safe passage from the north side to the south side where the subsurface topography is deeper."

Luigi responded: "I agree, but if they were to stay on the north side, and close to the shoreline, they would eventually have to turn north and even back west a bit to stay close to the shoreline. Frankly, it seems to be a stupid course setting, for there is nothing much of interest to see all the way up and into the Arctic Sea. If Prudhoe Bay was their intended point of interest, there are several much more efficient ways to get there."

Harold said: "He was, however, on the north side when the explosion occurred; so, what's your point?"

It was Paul who answered Harold's question: "I think Luigi might be on to something. If, for example, he was headed into the area by Shelikof Strait in the Gulf of Alaska, it is almost in a straight line from the Sea of Japan to be on the Aleutians' north side, until crossing the island chain at Akun Island. There is deep water there and an easy passage."

Linda asked: "What does that buy them?"

Connie, slowly nodding her head, replied: "They are now getting near some interesting areas; of course, you are near Anchorage, but even more interesting, you are also getting near Port Valdez and the Valdez Arm. There are several bays and ports along that area."

Linda asked: "Is the Valdez Fuel Port still active?"

Connie answered: "I don't know how active, but I am sure it is still there. Of course, the area is famous for the 'Exxon Valdez' tanker fuel spill that happened out in the bay many years ago."

Harold said: "Can we change the topic for a moment, and go back aboard the doomed Sub?

"As we look back at the incident, there are several areas where an explosion occurred, forcing the Sub to take the action it did. Putting that aside, what we don't know is, what items were aboard that Sub when it was forced to be scuttled?

"We know, for example, that there was a radioactive situation that forced everyone to the front deck, but did they have any weapons aboard, like missiles, etc.; if so, what were they.

"Because of the nature of the radioactive contamination, the actual deep-water sinking process was handled by two senior Russian crewmembers. Dressed in lead foil covering, they went back aboard the Sub and, from the front portion of the ship, were able to open all the sea doors to allow water to flood the cavities. As they left, they opened three hatches on the foredeck and two hatches on the sail. As the boat settled, water flowed in through those hatches and filled the interior.

"So, our people witnessed all this action, and it was our instruments that could verify that the vessel sank to the bottom in over five thousand feet of water. It is now lying on its side on the bottom."

Luigi said: "Yes, that is how the report reads, and we know that none of the Russian sailors were able to take anything with them as they were rescued."

Paul said: "So whatever was aboard the Sub is still there, and we know it can't be accessed.

Harold said: "There is just too much we don't know. As Linda has pointed out a few times, we need to learn about the crew members. Who are they, where are they from, who they represent, and if there is anything else that we can find out?

"Hopefully, we will get a direction to follow from something we learn from that list. Until then, we are just guessing."

CHAPTER FOURTEEN

Monday, 8 April 2019
3709 Sunset Blvd. East
Beverly Hills, California

Aron Chamorro sat by his pool, sipping a Martini that his butler had brought him a few minutes ago. The telephone call he had received from Aberdeen, Scotland, ten minutes earlier, was a bit disturbing.

Chamorro, a well-known Hollywood movie producer and director, had only been home a few minutes when the call came through, and he almost didn't answer it. Now he wasn't sure if he would have been happier had he not answered it. But he still would have learned about it anyway, maybe just not as soon.

The call was from Christopher Bing, who had been a longtime friend and associate of Aron, and they both had a compelling interest in the success of the North Sea oil production business. Although Bing, as CEO of 'Deep Ice Oil,' maintained fifty-three percent ownership of the company, Chamorro owned twenty-seven percent and was an always-available source of additional funds if needed. The remaining twenty percent was in the form of publicly owned stock.

What had disturbed Chamorro was the information he learned from Bing's meeting with the Iranian diplomat in Switzerland. Of course, all the news had been about the Russian Submarine incident and their resulting embarrassment; but to learn that the Iranians may have known of it three months before it even occurred was not reassuring.

His thoughts went to the incident itself and the Russians' tremendous cost in the Sub's loss. But why had it happened in American territory? If what Bing had said is true, then the Iranians had to have some obscure control over the Russians, and that thought was disturbing.

Chamorro wasn't worried about 'Deep Ice Oil' losing business; that loss had already occurred when the Americans changed their political posture and had succeeded in increased oil and liquid natural gas (LNG) production two years ago.

Although 'Deep Ice Oil' had now recovered much of that loss, he still had used all his connections to try and get the Washington political machine to block the increases in production, but to no avail. The new American policy had changed, and the overall economy had exploded into a new and highly productive era.

With the United States now self-sufficient in energy and fuel production, 'Deep Ice Oil' was forced into a major competitive market, one they never had envisioned.

Along with the Russians, most Middle East suppliers of energy and fuel oil, needed by Great Britain and the European Union, became the new primary sources. Because of the competition, those suppliers had suffered a significant loss in their profits. Now they were looking to form alliances wherever they could.

So, when Bing told him of the Iranian proposal, he had very mixed emotions.

He certainly wasn't a fan of the Iranians, and the thought of them having any control over the market was not to be tolerated.

However, he wasn't a fan of the new American approach either.

Although it had proven successful and the American economy had bounded forward to new heights, he still wanted to be assured that his North Sea oil investment was secure.

Quietly Sitting there, his mind shifted to the current film he was directing: "The New World Wave." This film aimed to display a division in the future, resulting in a conflict of philosophy between generations. The plot displayed a destructive future of what the writer believed could happen all within one generation: The first situation was if a controlled socialist society took over all the growth and development policies. The second situation was if those of individual desires and hard work succeeded in growing within private industrial development.

Like the movie itself, the answer would remain a mystery.

Chamorro was of mixed emotions; he and many of his Hollywood friends were very much on the socialist path, but his fortune had been earned through good investments in strong industrial companies. However, most of his friends and associates had gained their wealth through luck, family inheritance, and acting in the film industry. Somehow, he didn't think their great wealth had been earned, just acquired.

However, their input had influenced his political mind, and, although not a strong advocate, he went along with it.

This Iranian proposed partnership was not anything he had ever envisioned. He found he couldn't get his mind around it and didn't know if he should agree to it or not. Thinking he could leave it up to Bing, since he had the controlling portion of the company anyway, and, by taking the weak way out, he couldn't be blamed for a poor decision.

However, there were several million dollars of his investment at stake. He was also the available banker for the company if they needed additional operating funds; so, maybe he should take a more serious position. Indecision was pulling at him, and he was forced to realize that he could be risking a lot on a new and unproven plan of action from the Iranians.

He then thought everyone around him, in his closed and private world, was very left-leaning in their politics, and yet the current success from the change in energy sources was counter to their way of thinking.

He went back to his thoughts of the film he was directing and decided that the writer had actually leaned toward the socialist way of thinking.

OK, he made his decision. A text message to Bing sealed his fate when he indicated that he felt they should agree to and follow the Iranian proposal.

CHAPTER FIFTEEN

Tuesday, 9 April 2019
U.S. State Department
Washington D.C.
Office of the DOS Spokesperson

Following his directive from NSIU, Rudy was trying to find available information regarding the Tehran civil uprisings. For some reason, he found that his interest in these riots was compelling.

The questions in his mind were: Why did such conflict seem to exist between the government and the population? And had the people now become more non-acceptant of the government's absolute rule?

The religious leaders who, in essence dictated the government's policies, were able to direct the military and police actions necessary to keep the population under control. They were, however, slowly losing their influence over the frequent unrest displayed by these civilian uprisings. Could it be that these were the beginning actions of an attempted coup d'état?

The State Department was following what was going on in Iran as closely as possible. However, the Iranian Rulers had instilled policies and actions that forced many nations, including the United States, to take and apply punitive trade measures against them.

Therefore, it effectively closed off any diplomatic relationships. As a result, most communication and directions could only be obtained through the filter of a few very select European or Arab embassies.

He determined that the latest information available would probably be at the State Department, and his only known connection there would be with Jane.

After placing a friendly phone call, he was now sitting in her small office on the second floor, talking to her.

She had obtained some information that showed the unrest in Tehran was much wider spread than was generally known. It wasn't just in Tehran, but over much of the country, and growing in strength. Seemingly, the economic situation over there had been slipping, and, at the same time, popular unease had been growing.

Rudy asked: "Is there a reason that their economy is slipping so much?"

Jane answered: "From what I've heard, although caused by many things, the largest reason is based on the reduction of crude oil they supply to the European Union markets.

"It seems that, over the past two years, when the United States crude oil and energy production increased, our American fuel import demands declined. With America's loss as a major customer, it resulted in a lower overall available need for fuel to be supplied by the Mid-East countries globally.

So, they were forced to become more competitive, and they had to cut their excessive profits and become more realistic in their economies."

Rudy said: "I have heard that before; but, am I to understand that those economic reductions are the reason for the civil uprisings in Iran?"

Jane answered: "I probably am not the person to ask, but my thoughts form along that line; it just seems logical for that to be a reason."

Rudy said: "I wonder if, with this unrest going on over there, that explains the reason this information, from the State Department, was added to the NSIU weekly briefing from DOD."

Jane said: "I don't know, but when I see the Secretary this afternoon, I'll ask him. He looks to all available sources for information, and he may want NSIU to be involved in this particular State Department research, but without necessarily involving the DOD."

Rudy, as he was getting up to leave, said: "Thank you, Jane; I understand, but it was a curious note that was included, and the admiral wants to know why we are on the need to know list."

Back at NSIU, Rudy walked upstairs and found Harold, Connie, and Linda in the break room, wondering what they should do next. Harold said: "Rudy, get yourself some coffee and tell us something that will help us move forward with these weird investigations we seem to be stuck with."

Rudy, a large man with a soft, gentle voice, surprising for a man of his size, said: "Are you asking me?

"I thought you all would be way ahead on that Russian Submarine incident by now."

Linda, with a wide smile, said: "Until we get some additional information, we are just tossing bean bags at a 'Corn Hole' game."

She no sooner got the words out of her mouth than Paul and Luigi walked in with a file in Paul's hand. He said: "Here is the list of Russian sailors from the Nikolayevich Kosinski. It was faxed to the admiral's office ten minutes ago."

As he handed it to Harold, he added: "There were thirty-six sailors aboard, twenty-eight of them were officers of varying rank, and the rest enlisted men."

Harold glanced at the twenty-two-page fax and handed it to Connie, saying: "Does it have the information we need to figure something out?"

After a few quiet minutes, Linda, who had been reading it over Connie's shoulder, said: "It seems complete, and there are individual home addresses included with the other information."

Connie said: "I am surprised, but it is even more complete than I believed it would be. There are even detailed medical reports for each sailor's condition since they were initially treated medically aboard the 'Charles of Alaska'."

It was Paul, an ex-ski patroller and EMT, who said: "I am not all that surprised, they were all exposed to a radioactive source, and a check for resulting problems would be a normal procedure."

Connie got up and said: "Let me go, and I'll get us each a copy of this list, and we can meet in the conference room in twenty minutes."

Harold said: "Go ahead, I have an appointment with Sally. She wants to run by me the layout of a project she is thinking about, before she will introduce it to the floor of Congress. I'll probably be gone for the rest of the day.

An hour later, as they were sitting in the conference room, it was Linda who finally said: "These sailors are certainly a diverse group. However, they all seem to be from Russia's southern area between the Caspian Sea and Georgia and even northwest toward the Black Sea. Even the Captain, he is from Derbent on the Caspian Sea.

Luigi said: "Don't you find it a bit strange that the entire crew is all from the same small, albeit a more developed area than anywhere else in the largest country on the planet?"

Paul said: "I agree with you, Luigi; I find it strange that no one is from anywhere near the Moscow or northwestern area, and although it is a bit of a stretch, no one is from the eastern coastal area by Vladivostok either. That is where the Sub's home port is located."

Connie said: "That, in itself, may not be too much of a stretch Paul; Nuclear Submarines, in general, are at sea for extended periods, so where the crew lives, when off duty, may not be a deciding factor in their assignment."

It was Luigi, who again suggested that maybe their home locations may be somehow connected. He said: "I know that we, here in America, are more likely to come from all parts of our country and backgrounds, but I find it interesting that the southern area between the Caspian Sea and the Black Sea is proportionally tiny to the rest of Russia.

"It is also in an area greatly affected by the breakup of the old 'Soviet Union'."

Linda said: "For most of us, that happened twenty-eight years ago when we were all young children. I, for one, don't remember anything about that time besides what I have read in history books."

Connie said: "I think that maybe we should take some time and look at this list and the full incident report, without each other's influence for a day or so, including you too, Rudy, if you are available. Maybe individually, someone can find an idea or direction that the rest of us didn't think of.

CHAPTER SIXTEEN

Tuesday, 9 April 2019
'Deep Ice Oil' Corporate Office
Aberdeen, Scotland
United Kingdom

C hristopher Bing sat in his office, looking out of the window at two small tankers tied to the pier that extended out into the inlet from the North Sea. Both tankers were sitting low in the water, as they had recently arrived with a fresh load of crude oil from his northernmost drilling platform, about sixty miles northeast of Aberdeen, and had not yet begun to discharge their load.

Bing was more comfortable than he had previously been, for he had called his friend and business associate, Aron Chamorro, in Hollywood, to tell him the details of the Proposal that he was given by Darvish Abthai, the Iranian attaché to Switzerland. Bing knew that Chamorro was weak-minded about international business affairs, and he was easily swayed, both socially and politically, by his Hollywood associates. But he was a good friend and source of available funding when necessary, and he always meant well.

His call resulted in Chamorro, about an hour later, sending Bing a text saying that he thought it was a good idea to agree to the Iranian Proposal. That was enough for Bing to decide that 'Deep Ice Oil' would not accept any such proposal.

He had from time to time, when unsure of a decision he needed to make that involved the company's business, asked Chamorro for his opinion, and each time he had taken the exact opposite approach. It had always turned out to be the wiser choice.

As he sat there, his mind drifted back to the Proposal from Darvish Abthai, after being advised by Boris Kanski to listen to him.

Questions continued to form in his mind:

●Why would there even be a connection between those two people? Kanski is Russian, and Abthai is Iranian; they are from competing countries.

●If Abthai's story, about knowing that the Submarine incident was going to occur three months before it actually happened, is true, why would he and Kanski want to let us know about it?

●Or, more to the point, what is Kanski's reason even to have any knowledge of the Iranian claim or Proposal?

●It doesn't fit with Russia's oil production and international competition for fuel supply. The Russians were embarrassed and economically hit with the loss of a Nuclear Submarine. But what does all of that have to do with the Iranian Proposal?

●Why would the Iranians want an arrangement with my company; when we are already, in essence, competitors?

●Something is very strange in these questions, and he began to wonder what he should do or if he should call someone?

●The conversation in Switzerland with Abthai placed him in an uncomfortable and possibly risky position. Both Kanski and Abthai would know what they told him, and by his refusing to go along with their proposal, are they setting him up for a big fall somewhere down the line?

It was not a position he wanted to be in, so he decided to let someone he knew at MI-5 in London hear the story.

About six years ago, he had met Nigel Donaldson when there was a problem with drilling rigs too close to each other in the North Sea.

Donaldson was a U.K. investigator from MI-5, looking at international assets dealing with crude oil supplies throughout the European Union.

Deep Ice Oil was doing well at that time, and everything was in order, so Bing and Donaldson had no problems with each other. Although it was only a brief investigation with a clean outcome, the two men got along, became friends, and respected each other.

Bing placed a phone call to him, and Nigel himself answered it; he immediately felt better. He knew that this man would listen to him, and it would also have the added benefit of the British Government now knowing that he and his company were not doing anything strange or illegal.

After a few minutes of general pleasantries, Bing told him everything about the phone call he got, from the Russian Kanski, and the subsequent meeting, in Lausanne with the Iranian Abthai. He then told him that he had decided not to accept the Iranian's proposal, for he did not trust it; and felt it would be a poor business venture anyway. Before he hung up the phone, he told Donaldson that he wouldn't make any statements to anyone or answer the proposal without first speaking with him.

Donaldson was curious about many of the same questions that had bothered Bing. But the only ones who would know the answers would be Abthai and Kanski. Why would Kanski, with this knowledge, want anyone outside of the Russian Government to know about this Iranian claim?

The obvious answer involved an action that could change Russia's position on the world stage. Even to the extent of fermenting a coup d'état.

He hadn't heard of any such potential action, but those things are usually kept very close and not revealed before they happened.

He thought about the common ground of world events that were displayed in all the various statements. The one universal common point was right there in front of him, crude oil supplies.

The United States had, over the past two years, become fuel oil efficient and largely independent within their own country, and thus had caused a significant shift in the supply chain throughout the rest of the world.

Russia, Iran, and many Arab countries had been the undisputed suppliers of crude oil before then, but now they were in a very different competitive market.

It was interesting that an incident involving a Russian Submarine was to occur in American territorial waters. It created a potential nuclear energy disaster, embarrassing the Russians and forcing the Americans to launch a detailed rescue mission.

MI-5's interest was first in the welfare of the United Kingdom's citizens and their economy. Ironically, the change in the fuel oil supply chain had both the effect of lower-cost fuel due to increased competition, and at the same time, that same increase in the competition had hurt some of the British suppliers, like 'Deep Ice Oil'. These changes had also affected the European Union but in somewhat different ways.

Approximately six months ago, Donaldson had received a telephone call from an old friend at the NSIU in Washington, Commander Harold Jarrett. That call, between friends, involved shipping activities in Hong Kong, something the U.K. still had a fair amount of interest in. The information he learned from Harold helped the U.K. to keep a closer watch on things coming from Mainland China.

Today, however, he hadn't heard anything from the Americans regarding the Sub Incident several months ago, yet knowing them as he did, he thought that probably they were investigating it with a fine-tooth comb. So, a phone call to his friend at NSIU was indeed in order.

CHAPTER SEVENTEEN

Tuesday, 9 April 2019
NSIU Headquarters
Washington D.C.

Harold walked into NSIU early Tuesday morning, after a busy afternoon yesterday with Congresswoman Sally Martin at her office. She had asked if he could help her look at the financing plan that she had been working on. She was to present it to the floor of Congress today.

When they finished the work, they went together to a great Italian Restaurant that Harold knew about, then on to an outdoor Country Music concert, where they could relax and enjoy some time with each other.

It had been a pleasant evening, one they both enjoyed, and they realized that being together for both work and a little relaxation was something they agreed they would try to do more often.

He entered the Break room for a cup of coffee and to see if there were any donuts just lying around. Yeoman Susan Gordon was on her way to his office with a note, and as she turned the corner in the hallway and saw him enter the room, said: "Good morning Commander, Sir, I have a message for you from Nigel Donaldson at MI-5 in England, and he would like to speak with you.

Harold took the note she gave him, smiled, and said: "Thank you, Susan, first get yourself some coffee, then please return his call and put him through to my office right away."

Ten minutes later, the call from Donaldson came through. "Harold, you old dog, how are you doing? Is anything new happening over there in the colonies?" Asked Nigel.

Harold said: "Wait a minute, you called me, so let me check if I still have a wallet, or is my coffee cold, or is there a bunch of British troops planning another attack on Washington?"

Nigel responded: "We tried that about two hundred years ago, and it didn't go all that well for either of us. I understand that the coffee you referred to is the colonial replacement for our proper tea."

"Oh yes," responded Harold, "English tea; the cure for all evil!"

Nigel couldn't help himself for laughing. He said, between chuckles: "OK, I admit it, I have missed our back and forth and am very glad to hear you still have a good sense of humor.

Anyway, I have a good reason to be calling you. Have you got a few minutes to hear what I've just learned today?"

Harold answered: "My coffee is hot, and I am sitting down; so, what is it that you have just learned?"

Nigel said: "It is regarding the Nuclear Russian Submarine situation that happened a couple of months ago."

Harold, with a sudden attentive tone in his voice, said slowly: "Yes, the Russian embarrassment, we had to save their necks when it went so bad for them."

"Well, yes, so I understand," said Nigel: "It seems, however, that the Iranians may have known about it happening several months before it even occurred."

"Oh!" Said Harold: "And just where did you hear that from?"

Nigel said: "Be quiet and listen, there is a North Sea drilling company called 'Deep Ice Oil' that operates out of Aberdeen, up in Scotland. The CEO, and principal stockholder, is a man named Christopher Bing; I met him several years ago during an investigation we had up in the North Sea. Anyway, Bing is uncomfortable with a call he received from a Russian contact he knows, Boris Kanski. Kanski suggested to him that he meet with an Iranian attaché to Switzerland named Darvish Abthai.

"It seems that the meeting took place, in Lausanne, about ten days ago. Bing says Abthai told him the incident was planned to happen several months before it actually did. The Iranian told him that the incident was created to hurt Russia's reputation with the E.U., by showing there was an embarrassing situation developing between Russia and the United States."

Harold said: "The embarrassment they felt was global, not just in the E.U."

"Of course," replied Nigel, "but the change in fuel export to markets, other than to America, has forced a shift in the world supply chain. With the E.U. and Great Britain as the primary customers for a reliable fuel supply chain, there is now strong competition for that market."

Harold said: "That should be good for the world's economy; it makes those oil-producing countries that were previously unrealistic and rather piggish, in their production practices, become more in line."

Nigel said: "Agreed, but that resulted in strange partnerships and alliances. For example, the Russian supply chain was forced to join with the Iranians to compete with the Saudi Arabians and the UAE for that lucrative western European market.

"I see," said Harold, "but what does that have to do with the Sub incident?"

Nigel said: "Bing told me, that Abthai told him, that if they could create enough problems for the Russians, Iran would move away from them as an alliance. However, Iranian production would be insufficient for the E.U. market without the addition of supply from a North Sea company, like 'Deep Ice Oil'.

"So, Iran proposed the formation of an alliance with Bing's company and termination of the one they have with Russia; that is after they create another incident between Russia and America."

"I need to think about this for a while," said Harold: "Frankly, it sounds a bit far-fetched to me."

Nigel said: "I too have doubts, but I believe Bing was upfront with us; because for the simple reason he is planning to turn down the Iranian proposal, and don't laugh, I believe he wants to be patriotic about it."

Harold said: "Nigel, you have brought us into an area that we both need to explore. You know our relationship with Iran is pretty much non-existent, and we know yours isn't much better. So, we will look into it, and I presume you will too. Let's keep each other informed wherever we can, does that work for you?"

"We will keep in touch," said Nigel as they ended the call.

After Harold hung up, he began to think of reasons for the proposal that was made to Christopher Bing. Until this point, the only foreign involvement with the Sub's problem had been Russia; now, it seems, the Iranians are introduced into the mix. Many questions formed in his head because now they were going to look into how that occurred.

He got up, headed to the conference room on the third floor, found it-empty, and started down towards the Admiral's office. As he passed Linda's office, he heard Paul and Rudy's voices, disagreeing with both Linda's and Luigi's.

He stopped at the door and listened in on their discussion for a few moments; stepped in and said: "May I interrupt your conversation so I can throw a monkey wrench into this whole situation?"

All four stopped talking, turned, and looked at Harold with a mix of ideas about what he was going to say.

"First," he said, "is Connie around?"

With those words no sooner out of his mouth, he heard: "If you turn around, you might find me right behind you." Said Connie.

Although Linda's office was a bit small for the six of them, they all moved around enough so that everyone could sit down.

Connie said: "So what has happened that you need all of us together?"

Harold answered: "Well, I just got a very interesting phone call from Nigel Donaldson at England's MI-5. He told me of a very interesting conversation that he just had with Christopher Bing, CEO of the 'Deep Ice Oil' company in the North Sea region.

"It seems that Bing had a meeting with an Iranian attaché to Switzerland about a week or so ago. In that conversation, the Iranian told Bing that Iran knew about the Sub incident three months before it occurred."

Five pairs of eyes just stared at him in dead silence!

Finally, it was Linda who said: "You have to be kidding! How did Iran get into this mess?"

Harold smiled, looked over at her, and said: "That was somewhat the same reaction I had when Nigel told me about it.

"It appears that Bing had called him and told him of the conversation he had in Switzerland because he was very uncomfortable with the proposal that the Iranian made to him."

Harold then told them about the proposal and that Bing had decided not to go along with it.

Rudy, who was unusually quiet, looked around at the astonishment on everyone's face and said: "Isn't this the second or third time some action that involves Iran has come before us in just a week or so?"

"Hmmm," hummed Luigi, "perhaps we ought to weigh in with what we know, or think we know, and see if there are any connections we haven't looked at."

Harold got up and said: "Let me find the Admiral, and if he is available, we can meet in the conference room in twenty minutes."

Connie was the first to get up and said, "I'll see you there."

CHAPTER EIGHTEEN

Tuesday, 9 April 2019
Taiz Street
Near the Old City Gate
Sana'a, Yemen

Ahmad Abd-El-Kader had returned from his trip over to Sharjah the previous week. He was getting ready for his evening meal when his cell phone rang. The call was from his cousin Naseem Sargon, a well-known cleric from Azerbaijan with direct connection to Iran and the ayatollah in Tehran.

Ahmad, at twenty-nine years of age, was a bit unusual for a young man in Yemen. He was educated, fair in complexion, reasonably healthy, and in reasonable physical condition. He had studied civil engineering in Riyadh, Saudi Arabia, and could work almost anywhere he wished. His Muslim faith was strong, and he would do almost anything his cleric cousin would ask of him. But he was born and grew up in Yemen, and that was his home.

Naseem asked him how he had created the damage to the tanks, and more important had anyone been able to see him do it?

Ahmad answered: "Their security wasn't difficult to get around; I told them I was there to inspect some of the loading going on with freight containers that we had sent through their port. They asked where I was from, and I showed them my passport from Yemen and was cleared right away.

"They didn't even question me as I ventured around the whole site, and when I noticed that they were preparing to load a small tanker from one of the loading tanks, I stood back and watched. It would take some time, so the man doing the loading went away in his truck, leaving the site unattended for a few minutes.

"It was simple for me to walk by the piping and close the tank vent line valve. I knew that would cause the tank to implode quickly, and when it began to collapse and was realized, I thought that the men trying to open the vent valve wouldn't pay much attention to any of the other nearby tanks. So, I was able to set a small delayed explosive into the vents of those tanks, and, as I left the facility, they exploded."

Naseem said: "Are you sure that you cannot be traced? What about security cameras and witnesses?"

Ahmad answered: "I had a plain white kaffiyeh (scarf) over my head while I was near the tanks, and replaced it with my Yemen plaid one as I left.

"Even if they think that it was me, I am from Yemen, where would they find me?"

Naseem was comfortable with the report from Ahmad and thought now would be a good time to have him travel to Russia, to meet with the Russian Captain 3rd Rank, of the Nikolayevich Kosinski, Dmitry Heilig.

It was Heilig, a Russian born and educated man from Volgograd, who, along with several crew members, had been the most severely affected by the radioactive leak.

Naseem Sargon is a well-known cleric currently at a large Mosque in Baku, Azerbaijan.

Two years ago, he moved to Baku to assume the duties and prayers as an Imam. Although he had been at the Volgograd Mosque for eight years, his allegiance always remained to the Ayatollah in Tehran, Iran. That loyalty soon took hold of his actions in Baku as well.

But it was when he still was in Volgograd that he met and became friends with Heilig. Although a firm believer in the Muslim religion, Heilig had been less open about his faith while on active duty in the Russian Navy. But with the uncertain political changes and power struggles currently occurring in Moscow, he felt that his faith might be his future.

Captain 1st Rank Mikhail Ziolkowski was also worried. He wondered about the Moscow government's inability to follow the path laid out by the CPRF leadership (Communist Party of the Russian Federation). He wondered if there was a coup d'état being formed.

Heilig and Ziolkowski had traveled together from Vladivostok after the Navy released them from both medical and exhaustive investigative interviews. Ziolkowski, also a devout Muslim, remained in Volgograd rather than going back over to Derbent, after receiving a telephone call from Naseem.

Throughout several months of questioning, the Russian officials still did not know how the radioactive leak, or what caused the initial explosion, had occurred.

Captain Ziolkowski was relieved of any further assignment until the investigation was complete; because he would ultimately be held responsible. The rest of the crew were also not to be reassigned until the final report was written. Heilig and two others were still recovering from radioactive exposure, and they would probably end up being discharged from the Russian Navy.

It had been Heilig and 'Glvany Starshina' (Chief Petty Officer) Nikita Metzer, who had been the ones to go aboard the Sub and open all the hatches to scuttle it.

Naseem thought that Ahmad could fly to Tehran then on to Volgograd to meet Heilig and Ziolkowski. The meeting was to assure they were secure in knowing that the senior Russian government was unaware of any Iranian involvement.

CHAPTER NINETEEN

Tuesday, 9 April 2019 – 9:30 A.M.
United States State Department
Washington D.C.

L CDR Connie Wall sat across from Admiral Walker, both of them dressed in uniform, in the State Department's conference room. They were quietly waiting for Secretary Weiss to arrive.

Yesterday afternoon, a phone call from DOS had requested that they provide an update regarding the investigation into the Russian Sub incident.

As several advisors, and Jane, entered the room, Jane immediately came over to meet Connie and wish her well in her new position at NSIU.

As the Admiral introduced Connie to Jane, it was apparent that they both immediately liked each other. Jane said: "I am so pleased to meet you, Connie, and from what I've heard, you are a natural at investigative skills and can keep those pesky Navy Seals you work with under control."

With a big smile, Connie replied: "It is a pleasure to meet you as well, Jane, and those people at NSIU are indeed very special; I am lucky to have been selected to join them."

At that point, Secretary of State Weiss, along with Defense Secretary Collins, and two additional advisors entered the room.

After a brief introductory comment from Secretary Weiss, he said: "Secretary Collins and I have both been trying to find reasons for the Sub incident, and, I admit we are still at a loss to explain exactly why it happened. So, since both DOS and DOD are involved, we thought that maybe we needed to talk about it jointly."

He turned to the Admiral and asked: "How are we doing with this Russian Sub question? And, have you been able to find anything definitive?"

The Admiral looked around the room and said: "If you are asking me how it happened, we do have some answers. If you ask who caused it or even why it happened, we also have some ideas and perhaps even some indicators; but any definitive proof has yet to be found.

"However, we are quite sure that, although the cost, both financial and diplomatic, to Russia is very high, we have all but eliminated any chance that it was an accident.

"Our investigation has taken us to almost every available expert we have in nuclear submarine construction, configuration, and the actual operational procedures for sailing it. Universally, the opinions of these experts exclude any chance of an accidental detonation. Therefore, someone did it deliberately.

"I have brought along with me, Coast Guard Lieutenant Commander Connie Wall. She has recently joined our staff over at NSIU and will help us with our ongoing investigations. It seems rather fortunate that she became available to us at this particular time. She was immediately assigned to and is currently involved with this case, very appropriate since it was the Coast Guard that was first on the incident scene.

Turning to her, the Admiral asked: "Lieutenant Commander, would you please fill everyone in on what we have learned so far?"

As an ex-teacher at the Coast Guard OCS, Connie was comfortable with the presentation she had prepared for this particular discussion.

She politely said: "Aye, Admiral, as we have said, it became obvious that something was happening that was either planned or created to cause an expensive embarrassment for the Russians.

"We have determined that an explosive device was placed on the top seal of the reactor casing, and, when activated, the seal broke and allowed a significant air-born release of radioactive material contamination. The preliminary determination we made of that fact is that the crew's exposure and subsequent contamination were almost non-existent, except for only three men, and they were not severely affected.

"An Acula-Class Russian Submarine has approximately thirty-six crew members, and from our expert's knowledge, they are spread somewhat equally throughout the length and width of the interior. If the explosion was accidental, it is inconceivable that only three men would have been affected, considering all of the crewmen were moved to the outside foredeck, without any exposure, after it had surfaced."

Defense Secretary Collins asked: "I see your point, and it does seem that it was planned. But, have you any information as to why it occurred in American Territorial waters?"

Connie answered: "That is continuing to be at the front of our investigation. For example, why were they on the northside of the Aleutian Islands and so close to the shore? And in treacherous waters? Also, where were they headed to? What were they trying to accomplish?

"We have many answers to those questions, but which one is the correct one?

"The thought that they were spying on us, or monitoring our communications, or mapping access routes near our shore, is truly almost laughable. All of those reasons are too easily explained away."

Secretary Weiss asked: "Has your team found anything that may lead to a real explanation?"

Admiral Walker said: "Yes, Sir, there is an indication that there may have been an intention to create an embarrassment, not necessarily for the Russians, but maybe for us.

There was a sudden murmur in the room at that statement. It was Secretary Collins who spoke up, saying: "Embarrass us, how?"

The Admiral looked over and nodded to Connie. She answered: "Well, Sir, when we were trying to determine a reason as to how or why the Russians were following the coastline so close, things like shoreline topography, available visual areas, even possible points of potential sabotage were just not feasible. However, by following a potential direct route, it becomes possible that there is a location where the selection of such a route would be effective.

"The area that fits best that scenario is near Anchorage, or even better, in the bay of Valdez, near where the Exxon Valdez disaster occurred thirty years ago. It is only a guess, but if they duplicated an oil spill in that area, the uproar would be deafening!

"That is only speculation, of course, but so far, we haven't found a better reason, and largely it is mute. Quite simply, it didn't occur, and it was the Russians who were embarrassed."

With that said, it was the Admiral who spoke, saying: "Since we don't know, we are looking into exactly who caused the incident. It seems unlikely that the Russian Government planned it, yet all the sailors aboard were Russian. Therefore, whoever did it seems to be working for someone else?"

Again, looking over at Connie, he said: "Please tell them of the information that we received from MI-5."

Connie, a little uncomfortable about this information, said: "Yes, Sir. MI-5 received a call from a North Sea Oil Company Executive, who reported that he had met with an Iranian attaché in Switzerland.

Discussion from that meeting indicates that it seems there is a possibility that much of this was preplanned. The Iranian attaché said that Iran knew about the incident three months before it occurred."

The Admiral then added: "MI-5 believes it to be reliable and factual, and are following that path in their own investigation. We are also following up on that information. As you can see, that does confuse the situation; but we shall continue to follow up on it with MI-5."

Thoughtfully, Secretary Weiss looked over at Secretary Collins and asked: "Do you have any intelligence that may help us find an answer?"

"None at this point," answered Secretary Collins, "but I have a bad feeling about this. I believe it would be prudent for us to put all of our resources onto it."

Secretary Weiss said: "State will do the same; can we assume, Admiral, that you will continue with your investigation as well?"

"Of course, Sir," said Admiral Walker.

CHAPTER TWENTY

Tuesday, 9 April 2019 – 1:30 P.M.
NSIU Headquarters
Washington D.C.

The early morning meeting, over at the State Department, was a sobering moment for Connie. In just a short time, she had transitioned from a position as an instructor at the Coast Guard OCS; into an active investigator involved in an international incident. This morning, along with Admiral Walker, she was asked to provide an updated briefing to both the United States Secretary of State and the Secretary of Defense.

When she got back to her office after the meeting, she sat quietly at her desk. She just stared at the picture on the wall; it was of the surf breaking onto a beach, while the impact of all this struck home.

The change in her life was profound. It was only nine years ago that she had graduated from the Merchant Marine Academy as a junior commercial shipping officer. In contrast, today, as an officer in the Coast Guard assigned to the NSIU, she gave a briefing to some of the most powerful men on earth.

That realization brought everything into focus; she now had a responsibility to assure what the team was doing was correct and complete.

Harold had told her exactly what the NSIU was charged with to accomplish, in the many projects it received, but it was this morning's meeting where the realization of its importance became crystal clear.

The items investigated could affect the very strength and safety of the United States. It is an awesome responsibility.

Linda knocked on her open door and smiled at the serious look on Connie's face and said: "I can see that you have become aware of the need to be very accurate and complete in our investigations."

With a slight break in her voice, Connie said: "Hello Linda, come in, and please sit with me for a few minutes."

As Linda sat down, she immediately understood what had struck Connie so hard, and again, she smiled and told her: "When I first joined the NSIU, I had come from an investigative background, as a state police officer. I already knew the importance and significance of what we were doing. It is not always easy to understand just how important an investigation actually is.

"But putting that aside, when I got here, the magnitude and importance of these investigations became almost overwhelming."

Connie said: "I do understand, but when I was asked, this morning, to explain what we have learned to two Cabinet Officials, I realized that I must not only know what I am saying is accurate, but the decisions that they may make, based upon what I report to them, could be influenced by the way I state it."

Linda said: "All of our backgrounds are quite diverse. When Jane was first here, she was fresh out of the Navy OCS and wasn't too sure of herself at all; and she didn't have the experience you have. I, too, wasn't sure of myself either, and I had several years' experience in law enforcement.

"What I guess I am saying is, the sudden realization of the importance of this unit hits all of us. Remember that the men who do the most dangerous fieldwork and foreign investigations are all navy seals, and they are extremely bright, strong, brave, and very patriotic.

"But Connie, you have a natural ability to speak clearly, accurately, and with the unquestionable strength that serves you well.

"I believe that you now are truly seeing how very close we are to each other. And that is where our overall strength comes from; we are all in this together."

Connie feeling relieved and a little self-assured from Linda's comments smiled and said: "Thank you, Linda, you have a keen insight as to what I was thinking, and I do realize that this group of people is far more than just fellow workers. They are more like a family and watch out for each other. I am so pleased to be a part of them."

A knock on the door from Paul turned their attention to him as he excused himself and said: "Luigi and Rudy have been working on the crew's backgrounds, and asked if we can all meet in the conference room at two o'clock this afternoon; does that work for you?"

The conference room with Connie, Linda, Paul, Luigi, and Rudy at two o'clock was quickly expanded with the Admiral and Harold's unexpected arrival.

It was Harold who said: "I am sorry to break in on your thought process, but I just got a report from Ira, over in the UAE, and I think it may have some impact."

The Admiral said: "Before we get into that, I just wanted to tell Connie that you did a superb job today with the briefing over at the DOS this morning.

"Secretary Weiss called and said that after hearing your report, both DOS and DOD are stepping up looking for any intelligence available from the CIA or any other source they can find. The big item for them is the question, who would want the Russians to destroy such an expensive ship? And what benefit was there for it to involve us, even as a rescue mission?"

Harold said: "I guess we are asking ourselves the same questions, so let's look at what we know. That brings me to Ira's report.

"The investigation of the tank explosions in Sharjah has positively been determined as sabotage.

"More than that, however, Ira and a UAE investigator found video recordings from several security cameras that show a man actually closing off the vent valve on the tank that imploded, and seemingly placing explosives into the vent lines of the two that blew up.

"Of course, it was the reason for the joint investigation requested by the UAE. But they also have determined a likely suspect. It seems that when the culprit finished the sabotage, he left the area and walked out the gate. But the camera showed that he changed his keffiyeh from a pure white one, worn by many men in the Emirates, to a plaid one before he got to the gate.

"The UAE investigator with Ira recognized the plaid pattern and believed it to be typical of the type worn by men in Yemen. A quick check of the records shows only one man from Yemen was at the site that day, a man named Ahmad Abd-El-Kader, from the city of Sana'a."

Harold sat back in his chair and added: "This is where it might become interesting. It seems that the UAE is very detailed in tracking visitors to their country and keeping records of them. They have this man's address and even some knowledge of his background."

It was Rudy who then quietly said: "Yemen is not a place where we have a diplomatic relationship, but they do share a border with Saudi Arabia. It may be possible that information about this man can be obtained through them."

Harold said: "We can try that, but getting back to the reason I am bringing this up; it is a fuel oil sabotage, and our Russian Sub investigation seems to be leaning that way also. So, before we bring Ira and his team back home, do you think we have anything they should look at, while in that part of the world?"

It was Paul who answered: "We don't have anything more than just some theories regarding our fuel oil supply system, so, at this point, bring them home.

"We have been looking at the reason the Sub was where it was when it blew the reactor cover, and are finding less and less reason for it to have been on the route it was on; unless it was to sabotage or create a problem with our fuel oil supply system."

Luigi said: "If that is true, and we are leaning towards that belief, there are two huge questions we need to solve. Number one, what, and where, was the activity that would be the sub's original intention to accomplish, while in our territorial waters? And, number two, why did the sub's crew sabotage and destroy their own ship, basically wiping out the number one question?"

Linda said: "That brings us back to the crew, and what was the common thread amongst them that would allow such an action?"

Connie spoke up at this point, saying: "A common thread, 'hmmm'; as you said, there must be one. But all we know at this point is that they all came from homes in the same relative area, Russia's lower southwest corner, between the Caspian Sea and the Black Sea."

Sitting quietly, Rudy was thinking about that particular area of Russia; it was a common location for several specific reasons.

The breakup of the Soviet Union, which happened in December of 1991, changed many areas, both heavily populated and remote. This southwest area was largely impacted by a fair amount of both resentment and joy, amongst the people, over the splitting of certain countries.

It is more densely populated than most other areas in Russia, often non-secular. Yet, several divergent religious beliefs, primarily either Christian or Islamic, have mutated much of the area into multiple various local neighborhoods and communities, frequently independent from one another. Although mixed, those southern areas near Azerbaijan tend to be more of an Islamic majority. In contrast, the areas near Georgia and those up towards Ukraine lean more towards a mixed Christian population.

As he thought about it, the conversation he had with Jane yesterday came to mind. The riots in Tehran, she had said, were happening over much of Iran, not just in Tehran. Iran shares a common border with Azerbaijan, and both are strong Shia Islamic countries. A question entered his head, was there a possible connection?

CHAPTER TWENTY-ONE

Tuesday, 9 April 2019
Communist Party of the Russian Federation (CPRF)
Office of the President
Moscow, Russia

The Russian head of naval operations, Victor Polanski, had received a summons to come to the President's Office in Moscow. He was very nervous about this summons, believing the time had now come that he must give a final account for the Nikolayevich Kosinski's loss. He knew a lot, but the actual reason for the loss was still unknown to him.

The meeting was set for nine o'clock in the morning. Polanski arrived ten minutes early, and he was greeted by a security guard who escorted him up to a large room next to the President's office. That formal greeting by security only deepened his anxiety.

The President and six advisors all entered the room as he was standing at attention off to the side.

The President sat down and invited everyone to sit, as well. He then said: "Director Polanski, I assume that you are not completely aware of the circumstances that bring you to this meeting today. Let me, however, relieve your mind. I understand that much of what has happened with the Nikolayevich Kosinski was kept away from your knowledge. However, I have determined that it now becomes necessary for you to know what has happened; simply because we are hoping you can become involved and help with our plans.

The President had been gaining political strength over the past ten years, and it seemed that he was secure in his leadership position and would continue to have control of the government.

With an ice-cold tone in his voice, the President said: "Three very senior members of central committee have in place a potential situation that we now have found untenable. In short, they are planning a coup d'état."

Polanski was shocked. If what the President just told him is true, then he was placed in a mandatory supportive position to the current leadership. There could be no other choice.

He didn't know what to say, so the only words that came from his mouth were: "A coup, Mr. President?"

Turning to one of his aids, the President said: "Tell the Director what we have learned and what we may need him to do."

As the President got up and walked to his office, his Aid answered: "Yes, Sir."

Turning toward Polanski, he said: "Almost five months ago, a plan was discussed, amongst the members of the Politburo, to find a way to curb the increased production of fuel oil supplied by the United States for their own consumption. It had, I am sure you know, caused a change in the world's suppliers, forcing much competition.

"Discussions between the Americans and the Fuel producing countries did little to ease the situation, so these central committee members began looking for a way to cause international condemnation of the Americans and disrupt their current political position.

"The plan they finally decided on was to create an oil spill near the location of the 'Exxon Valdez' oil disaster thirty years ago. It would cause an embarrassment for the Americans, and the world's climate control outrage would be enough to shut down most of their production."

Polanski said: "But I thought you were going to explain what happened to the Nikolayevich Kosinski, it wasn't anywhere near the Valdez area, and there was no spill.

Our orders were to sail north of the Aleutian Islands, making the

Americans believe we were on a spying mission. However, the Captain's official instructions were for him to sail along the coast and confuse the Americans who were tracking us. When they got near a location where they could sneak ashore, with a small team, they could remotely cause a disruption by sabotaging a small fuel transport line."

The Aid said: "Yes, those were the instructions the Defense Committee gave you. However, these Members, we call them the 'April Surprise,' directly contacted the Captain, and there was a separate instruction to instead create a significant spill in the Valdez area.

"What is unknown is how they convinced the Submarine's senior crew to sabotage the reactor and scuttle the ship. The result being, as you know, we have the embarrassment.

"The loss of the Submarine has been enough for this 'April Surprise' group to begin a motion for new leadership, and they are creating a separate party to bring that forward."

Polanski wasn't sure that he was being told everything, but he had little choice in the matter. He Said: "What is it that you think I can do?"

The Aid responded: "Our sources tell us that the 'April Surprise' group still wants the Americans to sustain the embarrassment of an oil spill. So, you will be getting an order to plan another similar program."

Polanski looked at the Aid and felt even more uncomfortable than before. He said: "Are you asking me to duplicate the attempt of creating an oil spill in the Bay of Valdez?"

The Aid answered: "No, that was never our intention. The instructions that led to the incident off Alaska came from them, not us.

"This time, however, we want you to handpick a crew that will include several specially selected security agents. We will then have them secretly made available to the Members for special instructions yet to be determined.

"We do want the Americans to face an embarrassment related to their advancement in fuel production, but in a different area than Alaska."

Polanski, a career Navy officer; and now as the head of the Russian Navy, was getting an instruction to create a situation against any Navy officer's better judgment. Once again, he realized that he was in a position that left him with no other choice.

He had not yet heard who exactly these Politburo Members, referred to as the 'April Surprise,' were, and began to realize that he needed to know that answer before he could continue.

Looking directly into the eyes of the presidential Aid, he said: "I will follow the instructions, but only after I know the names of all those who comprise the people of your 'April Surprise.'

"You must understand, I am first, and always, a Russian, and I directly answer to my superiors, but there is a point where I must draw a line, and that line now exists. The President is my superior!"

CHAPTER TWENTY-TWO

Wednesday, 10 April 2019
Russian Federation Council Building
Moscow, Russia

About eleven o'clock Wednesday morning, Boris Kanski walked into his office. He found a note on his desk asking him to call Captain Ziolkowski, the Captain of the ill-fated Nikolayevich Kosinski.

Upon returning the call, the Captain told Kanski that the entire crew was now at their homes, apparently cleared and waiting for new assignments. All except himself, of course, because he was still being held responsible for the loss.

However, Ziolkowski wanted to tell him that he had met with a man named Ahmad Abd-El-Kader, from Yemen, when he landed in Volgograd.

He told Kanski: "It seems that Abd-El-Kader, although from Yemen, is a cousin of an Islamic Cleric named Naseem Sargon who gets his orders directly from Tehran.

"This man from Yemen flew into Volgograd to keep me, and the two men, who were the ones who actually sank the Sub, together; so, we could receive new instructions. He did not say from whom."

Kanski listened carefully but was unimpressed. He had already known about the Iranian government's plan. He was told that they were getting ready for another incident, this time, directly on an American Oil Rig in the Gulf of Mexico.

Kanski's direct connection with the Iranian attaché Abthai, in Switzerland, was the communication link between Iran and the three Central Committee members who were attempting the power grab in Russia.

For nearly two years, the pressure from the western world economies had been affecting Russia's position in the world trade market. They were indeed forced into several alliances that they would not ever have wanted to be in. Now there was a chance that, with a change in the Russian Federation's leadership, they could regain some, if not all, their position of superior power.

Kanski told Ziolkowski that he would pass on the information; and that he should remain there, in Volgograd. He then ended the call.

Kanski sat quietly at his desk, thinking about the takeover program with which he had become involved.

He had never been comfortable with the current president, and yet he began to wonder what his escape would be if this attempt began to fall apart.

These men from the Central Committee, who he reported to, had come to him with a plan to take down American influence in the world markets in general, and their fuel market in particular.

Their program was in contrast to the economic policies of the current CPRF and was aimed at restoring most of the previous values of years past.

He began to question if he was in over his head. The plan to restrict the Americans didn't bother him; in fact, he supported it. But it was the attack on the CPRF leadership and an attempt to replace the president that he was so unsure of.

Kanski had been born and raised in Derbent, but when he went off to school in Moscow, the last few people, who comprised the rest of his family, had moved over to Georgia. Although he had been raised a Christian and was still, he had spent most of his life in an Islamic neighborhood. He had always remained friends with many of them, and they all got along with each other.

He closed his eyes and thought about ways for a potential disaster to strike the Americans that would not be seen as being caused by Russia.

The Iranian Abthai had indicated that he received instructions, from Tehran, to have some sort of an oil spill occur near one of the currently operating drilling platforms; off shore in the Gulf of Mexico by Mobile, Alabama. They wanted it to look as if the excessive increase in production was the cause of the spill, and was the result of poor safety measures.

CHAPTER TWENTY-THREE

Monday, 15 April 2019
NSIU Headquarters
Washington D.C.

The ten o'clock meeting in the third-floor conference room was again full. The team that had gone over to the UAE had returned late Friday afternoon and were fully rested after a nice quiet weekend back in Washington.

The Admiral wasn't there this morning. He had gone over to the DOD to meet with Secretary of Defense Collins. He also wanted to find if any further information about Iran's reported involvement had been obtained concerning the Russian Sub incident.

He learned that the CIA and the FBI had mobilized their people in Europe, with instructions to find whatever information they could, which would lead to verification of Iranian involvement with the Russian Submarine's incident. They were also now working together with MI-5 and the various intelligence agencies from France, Switzerland, and Germany.

The claim that Iran knew about such a major event several months before it even happened was worrisome to all of them. Although each of those countries had kept some diplomatic relations with Iran, there was very little trust.

Back at the NSIU conference room, Ira was sitting with Antonio, Peter, and David to go over the plethora of data they had collected in Sharjah.

The explosive experts from the United States and the UAE had determined that the sabotage performed on the fuel tanks was done by someone who knew the precise mechanics of those tank operations.

However, simple physics would require that someone know what needs to be done to damage one tank, causing it to implode; while also knowing and being prepared for what is needed for the other tanks to explode.

That meant that the perpetrator was educated, probably in engineering. The video recordings from the security cameras had shown enough for them to identify him and showed that he was from Yemen.

Further investigation revealed that although he had claimed, as he arrived, to be checking on freight containers that were being shipped to Yemen, the investigators checked, only to find no record of any freight going to, or from, Yemen anytime that month.

As they put all their information together, Ira took out a copy of the file the UAE investigators had given him. It concerned a man named Ahmad Abd-El-Kader, from the city of Sana'a in Yemen.

Relations between Yemen and most of their Arab neighbors were, at best, tenuous. So, the UAE investigators had sent a request to Riyadh, Saudi Arabia, for any information they might have regarding this man. The inquiry results came back to the detectives just before the NSIU team left to fly back to Washington.

In general, Saudi Arabia and the Riyadh authorities kept meticulous records of most people who have spent any time in their country. Almost immediately, the name of Ahmad Abd-El-Kader, from Yemen, popped up.

The file showed that he was a young man born in Yemen in 1990. His parents raised him in Sana'a, where his father was a language translator for the local city government. His father's influence in languages was what probably enabled him to learn and speak fluently five languages, Arabic, Farsi, French, Russian, and English.

He had attended the Riyadh College of Technology for four years and had graduated with a degree in Civil Engineering Technology.

His engineering and linguistic education allowed him to work and live almost anywhere he chose in the Arab world. But Yemen was his home and, although one of the poorest countries on earth, that is where he wanted to be.

The only living relative that appeared on his record was a cousin named Naseem Sargon, who was listed as an Islamic cleric in Baku, Azerbaijan.

As Linda, Paul, Luigi, and Rudy came in, sat down, and opened their notebooks, Linda said: "It is good to see you all back in one piece. How was the trip?"

Peter, nodding to Linda, answered: "Sharjah is a special place, although mostly desert, along the coast it is really quite beautiful. They have built islands, out into the Persian Gulf, that look like palm trees from the air. They have built hotels, condominiums, and even private homes out on the branches, where tourists and business people live and stay. It is indeed, unique."

Ira said: "Of course, we were there for a different reason, and I must say, we were looking at a strange circumstance."

Antonio spoke up, saying: "Ira is right, it was strange, but we know for sure it was sabotage, and we believe we found the identity of the culprit.

At that moment, Harold and Connie entered and sat down. Harold said: "It is good to see you guys back here. Is everything OK?"

Antonio said: "We are all fine, but there will be questions as to where we go from here."

Then while passing his copy of their report over to Harold, he continued: "We know how it was done, and we are even sure we know the individual who did it, but he is from Yemen, and neither we nor the UAE has access to him. Before we left, we asked if the neighboring Arab nations would place him on a watch list. They said they would do so, but those countries' political atmospheres are not very interested in Yemen."

Ira added: "At this point, we can do nothing else. However, the UAE is a little aggravated about their tanks' being sabotaged and will push as hard as possible to find any connection that this man had with Iran. That is where they feel this attack originated."

Rudy sat up straight at that comment, looked over directly at Ira, and asked: "Iran, what makes them think he has a connection with Iran?"

It was Peter who answered: "The records kept by the Saudi's are quite complete and, I don't know how they do it, but they keep them right up to date. Although he lives in Yemen, this Ahmad Abd-El-Kader has only one known living relative, a cousin named Naseem Sargon, an active Islamic cleric in Baku Azerbaijan. It is apparently well understood that the clerics in Azerbaijan closely follow directions from the ayatollah in Tehran."

Paul and Luigi looked at each other and could read the thoughts in each other's minds. It was Paul who said: "It would seem that Iran is finding its way into several of our current investigations; perhaps they are all connected."

Harold said: "It does appear that something is happening that may have begun in Iran.

"To put all of us on the same page, I will tell you that, as you were returning from the middle east, our investigation into the Russian Sub incident has expanded.

Last Tuesday, Nigel Donaldson, across the pond at MI-5 in London, called me. He told me that he had just received a phone call from a North Sea Oil Company executive that he knew. It seems that this executive had been advised by a Russian named Boris Kanski, from Moscow, to meet with an Iranian attaché in Switzerland named Darvish Abthai.

"This all took place about two weeks ago, and the executive did meet with this Abthai. At the meeting, he was offered a strange business proposal that would have Iran partner with him in fuel distribution, replacing their current deal with the Russians. He mentioned, during the conversation, that Iran knew about the Russian Sub incident three months before it ever happened. That, of course, means they were somehow involved with it."

With a thoughtful look on his face, Luigi said: "Is it my imagination, or have we a new direction to go in?

"First, we have the Russians embarrassed, then the UAE has sabotage done on their fuel tanks, and now, added into the mix, is a British Oil Company being positioned to replace the Russians in the fuel supply chain.

"That, when left alone, is almost understandable, until you add the fact that the Russians, or at least their own Russian sailors, destroyed their Nuclear Submarine while in American territory. And that, ladies and gentlemen, leaves us to wonder; why are we involved in any of this?"

Connie, who hadn't said a word since entering the room, smiled at Luigi and said simply: "My thoughts exactly!"

CHAPTER TWENTY-FOUR

Tuesday, 16 April 2019 – 8:30 A.M.
NSIU Headquarters
Washington D.C.

Linda walked into her office and sat down at her desk. She looked at her coffee cup and saw that it was empty, probably because she forgot to fill it.

From the open door, Connie asked: "May I sit with you for a minute?"

Linda looked up, smiled, and said: "Of course, but I forgot to fix my coffee. Do you want to walk down to the break room with me?"

Connie, completely aware that Linda's mind was off somewhere in space, said: "Sure, I need one too."

Once they had fixed their morning coffees and took a sip, Connie said: "I think that you are off in thought somewhere, and, I guess, I am too. So, I wonder if we are thinking about the same thing?"

Linda said: "Why are we involved in any of this?

"That was what Luigi said yesterday, and it has stuck in my head.

"He is right! What are we missing?

"I woke up early this morning thinking about it, and now I want to find out."

Connie said: "I didn't lose any sleep over it, but what we have talked about for the past week does bring that upfront. I have thought about asking someone who is not involved; someone, not necessarily in the military or connected with the government, just a person with a fresh perspective.

"My problem is, I really don't know anyone like that, and thought that you, as a civilian, just might."

Linda said: "You know, Connie, your mind works a lot like mine; I had a very similar idea. The fact is, I do know a trucking executive in New York who is very astute and is connected with several very bright friends and associates who might be willing to talk to us."

She went on to describe: "About a year ago, we were looking into a China issue, and I happened to meet these people about an impact that was possibly going to occur in our agricultural industry. We became friends, and they were very helpful.

"I will call him and ask if we can meet with them. Are you up for a train ride to the big apple?"

John Carrick, Associate Director of Central U.S. Trucking Corporation, had just arrived in his office when the call came through from Linda. He hadn't heard from her in a while and was delighted to find she was doing well and wanted to see him.

"Linda, how nice to hear from you," he said: "What brings this delightful surprise to me early this Tuesday morning?"

Linda answered: "Good morning John, I was just thinking that I seem to have gotten lost in several problems we are working on, and thought, if you are free for a little while, I'd like to come up to New York and get your perspective on something that has us befuddled."

John answered: "It was about a year ago that you and I chatted with Annie, Emilio, and Gene about something strange that was going on then. I admit it was fun to think about it, and we all learned a lot from our discussions."

Linda said: "I totally agree, and now we find ourselves looking for a fresh perspective on a current investigation.

"I was telling another of our investigators, Connie Wall, that we needed to clear our minds and find someone who might see the forest through all the trees. You guys came right to mind, and I told Connie that just maybe, if I offer to buy lunch for everyone, we might be able to meet today and pick your brains."

John said: "It is short notice, but I'll call you right back, let me ask them." And, without waiting for a response, he hung up.

Exactly eight minutes later, her phone rang, and John told her they all were excited to meet for lunch at 12:45 P.M. He said that she and Connie should come to his office at 12:30 P.M. and he would take them to the Austin Steak House where they have a reservation.

Then he said: "Don't worry, we played rock, paper, scissors again, and this time Emilio lost and he is buying!"

With a short note to Harold, explaining their quick trip, Connie and Linda had to hurry, and just caught the new express Amtrack high-speed train to New York City with just fifteen minutes to spare.

As they entered the Central U.S. Trucking Corporation's main Lobby, they were met by a secretary who greeted them and told them that Mr. Carrick would be right with them.

Two minutes later, the elevator door opened, and John came right over and gave Linda and Connie a welcoming smile, saying: "I am looking forward to this afternoon, it is so nice to see you again, Linda.

Linda, turning to Connie, said: "Connie, this is John Carrick, and John I'd like you to meet Connie Wall."

John said: "Ms. Wall, I am pleased to meet you and hope you will enjoy your visit with us."

Connie said: "Please call me Connie. I am getting used to the very pleasant familiar atmosphere of true society."

Linda broke in and said: "John, I'm sorry, but I should have properly introduced Connie; she is Lieutenant Commander Connie Wall of the United States Coast Guard."

John said: "Well, I am honored, Connie, and please call me John."

With the two ladies, one on each arm, he said: "Shall we go meet the others?"

As they arrived at the Austin Steak House, Linda was pleased by the greeting she got from Annie, Gene, and Emilio.

Annie Selene is a junior executive for a major international banking conglomerate; Gene Elbridge is a trading broker on the New York Mercantile Exchange (NYMEX); Emilio Watson is the director of Pacific Ocean shipping coordination for the International Ocean Shipping Company (IOSC).

After John introduced Connie to them, they were all guided to a large round table in a private room near the restaurant's back.

It was Annie, who right away said: "OK, so please tell us how you, Connie, a Coast Guard Officer, are assigned to the Navy; the NSIU is a Navy group, isn't it?"

Linda, couldn't hold it in; she burst out laughing, which had the effect of getting everyone else laughing at the same time. She said: "Annie, you never fail to amaze me. You asked me a similar question when we first met over a year ago."

Connie, with a big smile, answered: "Well, Annie; it seems that Admiral Walker, at NSIU, needed a new assistant. He and his old college friend Admiral Hicks, commander of the Coast Guard Officer's Candidate School, set me up for an impromptu interview without my knowledge.

"I'd been an instructor at OCS for seven years and was completely surprised. Quite simply, I found myself in Washington by the end of that week as a Coast Guard Officer attached to the U.S. Navy! I agree it is a bit weird. However, I have never worked with a better or more dedicated group of people in my life; I wouldn't ask for anything different."

John said: "Are we all pretty much loose for the rest of the day?"

Annie said that she had nothing urgent on her schedule, Emilio echoed that sentiment, and Gene said the NYMEX was following a dead slow day; unless he got a call, nothing was exciting going on there.

It was Linda who said: "Well, first I want to thank you guys for meeting with us. Besides an excellent lunch with friends, there is something strange that we are looking into.

"I am sure you saw the news a few months ago, regarding the Russian

Submarine incident off the Aleutian Islands. Well, we have been looking for any reason that it happened in American Territorial waters. That is our assignment, but we keep finding things that make us wonder why is America even involved?

Emilio said: "That is an interesting question. As you might remember, we are a Pacific Ocean shipping company, and several of our Asian Routes follow a line south of those Islands. It occurred to us, at the time, that we were lucky not to be very near those islands when the incident happened. We didn't think much about it at the time, but I wonder why they hadn't taken a more direct route to the north in international waters."

John said: "Alaska in the north Bering Sea is, for the most part, pretty sparse. Any idea what would make them want to go there?"

It was Gene who answered right away with one word: "Oil!"

Annie said: "What do you mean by that?"

Gene said: "Well, Alaska is famous for two big discoveries in the last hundred and fifty years, gold and oil. I think we can agree that the gold rush is pretty much over, but crude oil drilling and transport are continuing in abundance."

John added: "The transport of crude oil from Alaska to the United States mainland has become an increasing available source of energy over the past two years. Of course, the supplies from the drilling platforms in the Gulf of Mexico stretching from Galveston, Texas to Mobile, Alabama, are just as productive.

"But why do you think, Gene, it might have been the reason for the Russians to be where they were?" Asked Linda.

"I don't know about that," said Gene, "but as you know, we trade Crude Oil futures contracts on the Mercantile, and the overall price has declined as the United States has become more self-sufficient over the past two years."

Annie said: "But with America increasing supply, why is the market declining?"

Gene answered: "Because America isn't the only source of crude oil, and as we purchase less and less from foreign sources, the middle east and the eastern European suppliers are feeling a loss in profit due to increased competition. Quite simply, they have lost the source for a large portion of their income. And don't forget, many of the investors who trade in the futures market are from that part of the world."

Connie said: "But it was a Russian Submarine that was lost; how does that affect the United States? We saved their crew and, politics aside, helped stabilize a dangerous situation. And I understand that Russia is one of the largest suppliers of crude oil in the world."

Emilio answered: "I see Gene's point, and to answer your question Connie, the Russians are also likely to lose even more income as a result of the embarrassment that they have suffered."

It was Annie who then said: "If the world's oil producers are looking to regain their market share, they need to decrease the capability of their largest consumer, the United States, to produce its own supply of crude oil. That means that they need to cause a situation that would accomplish that goal. What comes to mind?"

Linda looked over at Annie with new respect and said: "You are correct, Annie; if America has an accident or disaster that causes an environmental catastrophe, like a major oil spill; without a doubt, the world's conservationist will pile on condemnation.

"We have thought about that. But with the added factor of foreign investors making future trades that drops the market value of crude oil, the object of reducing the competition, necessary to restore those markets, means that it may go beyond just the United States as the primary target."

Connie looked up at Linda and read her mind, realizing it had already happened with the UAE's fuel tank sabotage!

It was John who then said: "I think I would look very closely at the many platforms we have in the Gulf of Mexico; they seem to be the most vulnerable target."

CHAPTER TWENTY-FIVE

Wednesday, 17 April 2019 – 9:00 A.M.
Russian Federation Council Building
Moscow, Russia

Boris Kanski was getting nervous. Normal communications, and discussions, that frequently were passed around through the Central Committee members' staff offices had become quiet for some reason. Even communication from the three men he reported to had become less frequent and less informative than before.

Kanski, as a senior advisor for these committeemen, committed himself to the proposed takeover of the CPRF leadership. But now it was almost as if he was being set up to take the blame.

What had happened? Something was wrong; he could feel the tension growing as the days passed.

He had followed instructions and given private orders to Captain Ziolkowski, of the Nikolayevich Kosinski, to destroy his Submarine while in American Territory, causing a severe embarrassment to the CPRF president.

He didn't ask how the Central Committee members knew he had a connection with the Iranian Abthai, but somehow, they knew; and used him as the conduit to Iran's leaders.

He had arranged it so that the crew, all from the Volgograd area, would follow the orders of Captain Ziolkowski and his associate, Captain 3rd Rank Dmitry Heilig.

All had gone as they had planned, but now something was wrong. The CPRF president was still in power and maybe even a little stronger. The silence from the Central Committee members, along with the Naval Director Polanski's continuation as the Navy's supreme head, could only mean that the president and his aides were getting ready to disclose the attempted coup.

His thoughts went to his home. He lived in an apartment with a woman that he had been with for eight years. She was a secretary in the offices of a popular magazine publisher. They had become attached, but they never even thought about marriage. If he left, she would be OK.

Today is Wednesday. He thought no one would miss him before Monday, so that would give him almost five days before anyone with authority would come looking for him.

He picked up his overnight case, the one he always kept at the office, slipped his laptop computer into its case, and locked his office door as he left.

As he walked by the park behind the square, he stopped and stepped into the little bakery to his right. After purchasing a roll and a cup of tea, he walked out the back door to the adjoining street and climbed onto the passing trolly. The simple, quick unexpected movements, assured him he was not being followed. Twenty minutes later, he was at the Kievskiy train station by Kievskiy Square.

It was crowded inside the station, and he stood in line to purchase a ticket. It moved quickly, and he purchased a round trip ticket to Volgograd. Round trip tickets aren't looked at carefully, so he didn't even have to show any identification. He had ten minutes before the train was to leave, so he entered the Restroom, and while no one was around, removed the battery from his cell phone.

It was a strange feeling for a Russian Communist Party government employee, for there was now no one who would know who or where he was.

Seven and a half hours later, Kanski stepped off the train in Volgograd Railway Station. As he walked across the lobby, he felt safely anonymous for the first time in years.

A local Taxi took him to a small hotel on the south side of the city. When he was checking in, the desk clerk asked for his identification. He knew that was going to happen, so he took out his CPRF badge and quickly showed it to the clerk while making sure his fingers covered the name and number on it. The clerk's eyes opened wide at the sight of a Central Committee CPRF Badge but knew enough not to question it.

Once he got up to his room, he used the hotel telephone to call Ziolkowski and set up a meeting with him at a local restaurant in two hours.

After he hung up, he thought that just maybe, he ought to let someone know what was going on, someone who knew what had already happened, and what the planned situation between Russia and Iran was.

He didn't hesitate and put through a call to Christopher Bing in Scotland.

The conversation was short. Although Bing listened to Kanski's description of the Russian & Iranian plan, he said nothing about the proposal he had gotten from Abthai in Switzerland; and he made no mention of his conversation with MI-5 in London.

Kanski felt uneasy after speaking with Bing. He knew, although everything that could be done had been done, there was still a chill in his bones when he thought about it.

He decided to walk to the restaurant for his meeting with Ziolkowski. It was only eight blocks away and across the park; that way, he would take some time to relax his mind.

The early evening air was full of mosquitoes. They seemed to be everywhere, and they swarmed around his head while he was walking past a pond filled with very still water. He hadn't gone three full blocks before he was stung on his neck by one. He slapped at it and picked up his pace, hoping they would leave him alone.

Ten minutes later, he was at the restaurant, sitting at a table with a glass of vodka, waiting for Ziolkowski. As he saw him enter the front door, he stood up to signal where he was; when, without warning, everything went dark. He collapsed to the floor, stone dead.

Ziolkowski saw him collapse and, without hesitation, turned around and walked back out of the restaurant and down the street.

Within five minutes, an ambulance pulled up in front of the restaurant. Two men sitting across the street in a gray sedan looked at each other, smiled, and watched as Kanski's body was carried out and placed in the waiting ambulance.

The man sitting in the passenger seat took out his cell phone and placed a call to Moscow. Within five minutes, the report on Kanski's removal was sitting on the president's desk.

As the two KGB agents pulled away from the curb, the passenger placed the almost invisible dart gun back into its case.

CHAPTER TWENTY-SIX

Thursday, 18 April 2019
NSIU Headquarters
Washington D.C.

Harold came into his office and stood still in the middle of the room. He hadn't had a chance to talk with anyone about the Sub incident for several days and began to feel a bit left out. Of course, the fact that he hadn't been around the NSIU building since Monday might have something to do with it, but he still felt as if he just wasn't up to date.

Tuesday and Wednesday, he had taken a little vacation with Congresswoman Sally Martin. They had gone off to visit with a couple of his friends at their beach house in Avalon, New Jersey.

Carol and John, Harold's friends from New York City, were on a week-long Spring break and had invited both Harold and Sally to come over to Avalon, relax and stay with them for a couple of days.

They had known Harold for many years but had only met Sally at a Country Music concert they all had attended a few weeks ago.

They saw how easily both Sally and Harold got along with each other.

It was evident to Carol and John that Harold and Sally both had brilliant minds and needed to relax them every so often. It was also evident, particularly to Carol, that they were becoming infatuated with each other but were trying hard not to admit it.

Somehow, she knew that Elsie, their sweet old Golden Retriever, would have the effect of bringing them to the realization that they needed to be together; simply by just lying on the floor between them when they were sitting and relaxing.

As they were chatting about the news or the latest country music awards, Carol, hiding a slight smile, noticed that each of them would drop a hand to scratch Elsie behind her ears every few minutes. Elsie, with her eyes closed, was just lying there, in heaven, with all the attention.

Today, however, Sally had gone back for arguments being discussed on the floor of Congress, and he was back at NSIU thinking about the incident.

"How was your short vacation with Sally over in Avalon?" Asked Linda from the door.

Harold's face turned a little red, and he said: "Very nice, it was good to see old friends."

Then with a sly smile, said: "How was your trip up to the big apple? And what is new with John Carrick?"

It was Linda's turn to get a red face, as she answered with a smile: "It was an interesting trip, and, yes, I enjoyed seeing John again. How did you know we went up to New York on Tuesday?"

He answered: "I have my ways!"

She looked at him with her eyes wide open, shook her head, and said: "Anyway, we learned a few things and got a couple of ideas. Should we all meet at ten o'clock upstairs?"

As he was going to say yes, his phone rang. So, nodding agreement to Linda as she left his office, he picked it up. Yeoman Susan Gordon had a new message from Nigel Donaldson over at MI-5, asking him to return his call.

As it was getting near ten o'clock, everyone was finding their way upstairs to the Conference Room. Once again, when the whole seal team is in town, the room seemed crowded. But everyone was thinking about the incident and was anxious to find out something they could dive into.

Connie and Linda started the discussion with a report on their quick trip up to New York.

Linda said: "On Tuesday morning, Connie and I were in her office trying to come to grips with your comment on Monday, Luigi.

"Do you remember saying: 'Why are we involved in any of this?'

Well, both Connie and I both started to think the same way and figured that you are right; why are we involved in any of this?"

Connie picked up on the subject and said: "So I asked Linda if maybe we are just too close to all of this, and, to use that old saying, maybe we cannot see the forest for all of the trees."

"We agreed that we needed a fresh view of the situation, from someone who isn't directly involved."

Linda said: "We are all too close to the problem here, so I got to thinking why not ask those people in New York, who were such a big help when we had the China Nuclear issue last year, for their input and opinions.

"When it all comes together, it usually involves something to do with the economy, and those guys are deep into it."

Connie picked up the narrative, saying: "And it is as we thought, they believe that our country's ability to produce our own crude oil and transport it, has made the world's fuel oil economy decline in profit, as a result of increased competition."

Luigi said: "Well, yes, but we already knew that."

Then Connie added: "But it is more than that, the investors around the world trade in the future prices of the crude oil, and they have suffered quite a decline in value. So, their goal is to regain that edge, and that comes from causing America to produce less and again buy it from foreign sources."

Paul, who had been quiet all morning, said: "I see, they need for our country to have something happen that will force us to stop our self-production of crude oil. Making it necessary for us to buy it from them."

Linda said: "Exactly!"

Antonio asked: "Did they have any suggestions on how that could happen?"

Linda answered: "We talked about that, and they all almost together said that if we had a major spill, environmental condemnation and embarrassment would shut us down."

Connie said: "John Carrick mentioned that he thinks we are most vulnerable with the drilling platforms in the Gulf of Mexico. They would be the easiest place to cause a big problem.

"Both Linda and I agree with him."

Admiral Walker had come into the room when the discussion had turned to the economy, and he just quietly stood aside listening. The one thought still in his mind was the cost the Russians had paid for the Submarine's loss, and it was still that they were the ones who were embarrassed. Even with the newly discovered participation of the Iranians in it, it was still the Russians who had taken the brunt of it.

As the door behind him opened, he turned to look at Harold as he entered the room. There was a strange look on his face as he stopped next to the admiral. Then, as they both gave a slight nod to each other, strode over to the table and sat down.

The room was quiet, as everyone was waiting to hear what Harold had learned.

He said: "Sorry I'm a bit late, but I just got off the phone with Nigel Donaldson. He told me that he had gotten another call from that North Sea oil executive that he knows, Christopher Bing, and it was quite revealing.

"It seems that a very senior aid and advisor to three very senior Russian Central Committee members, Boris Kanski, a name we have heard before, called him yesterday afternoon from Volgograd in southern Russia.

"What makes that call interesting; was that Kanski told him that the plan with Iran to cut off the Russian alliance, with the oil trade, was no longer an issue. However, apparently, Kanski felt betrayed by his superiors, and he had gotten out of Moscow before they could get him and place all the blame for the Sub incident on him.

"He said he was safe in Volgograd for the moment, as no one knew where he was. He was going to call the Sub's Captain, who he knew needs to escape as well. If he could arrange it, together, they would get out of the country tomorrow and go south to Baku in Azerbaijan. His reason for telling Bing all this, he said, was to have someone who couldn't be touched know that he was now out of it. He also advised Bing to think carefully before making any deals with the Iranians, at least until he spoke to him again.

"Harold looked around at everyone then quietly said: "While I was on the phone call with Nigel, he asked me to hold on for a moment, as he was getting a faxed printout report from one of their agents in Volgograd.

"The agent didn't say how he knew it, but he had just learned that a senior Central Committee Aid had died while in a restaurant last night at about eight o'clock. The body was identified as Boris Kanski, and there was a tiny pinhole in his neck behind his right ear.

Nigel told me that their agent in Russia indicated that this had become a common method of delayed poisoning, used by the new revised KGB, to remove someone who has become politically dangerous to the CPRF.

The room was silent, and everyone was looking at Harold, letting the report he had just given sink in.

After a few moments, it was Ira who said: "Well, where does that leave us now?"

There was no answer from anyone until Antonio spoke up, saying: "OK! We know that the Submarine was in American Territory when the incident occurred. We know, or think we know, that it was a planned event. We know, or think we know, who planned it. We know, or think we know, that it was part of a larger plan to hurt our fuel oil production, thus changing the world's economy. We know, or think we know, that we are the likely target of another attack. We know, or think we know, that Iran is directly involved.

"I could go on, but the question really is: Do we know enough, or can we prove enough, to write a final report to the DOD and closeout this investigation?"

Again, there was a long silent pause until Admiral Walker, with a slow, soft tone in his voice, answered: "No, we are not ready. I hate to say it, but although Antonio has outlined it quite well, we must know what is likely to occur, hopefully before it happens. We must find out what that is, so that when we give the report over to DOD and DOS, Secretary Collins and Secretary Weiss will have enough to place some type of restriction, or counteraction, perhaps against both Russia and Iran, or whomever they deem responsible."

CHAPTER TWENTY-SEVEN

Thursday, 18 April 2019
Volgograd, Russia

Soon after Captain Ziolkowski had witnessed Kanski's death, he realized that he, too, could be in a lot of trouble. Although he immediately had stepped out of the restaurant, without anyone seeing him, he realized he was being set up to be the one who would be blamed for the entire incident.

That fact became clear to him when he had learned, yesterday, that the head of naval operations, Victor Polanski, was still in that very powerful position.

Both Ziolkowski and Heilig had followed Polanski's current orders, from naval operations, to remain available in Volgograd. But when Ziolkowski witnessed what happened to Kanski, he now knew that no one would believe he had been given a specific order to destroy the Nikolayevich Kosinski.

Therefore, he decided that his only chance was to disappear.

Captain 3rd Rank Dmitry Heilig was also going to be in trouble. Still, even though he knew about the plan, he was more of a hero for getting the crew to safety and ultimately being the officer who went back aboard the contaminated Sub to scuttle it.

It had been Ziolkowski who ordered the explosion on the reactor cover, and the only one who knew about it was Heilig, and it was he who had gotten the crew to safety before detonating it. In both their cases, their protection from discovery was Kanski, and he was now dead.

A few days ago, Ziolkowski had met Ahmad Abd-El-Kader when he arrived in Volgograd. They had a short discussion, where Ahmad assured him that the CPRF president did not know about the arrangement between Kanski and the Iranians. However, after seeing the killing of Kanski last night, the Captain wasn't so sure.

He walked, thinking about what to do, and figured that he needed to tell someone what he had witnessed. He called Ahmad at his hotel and told him about the assassination of Kanski.

Ahmad, who was not involved with any planning or details, only did what he was instructed to do by his cousin Naseem. So, after hearing from the Captain, and with this new information, he called his cousin to ask for instructions.

When Naseem got the call from Ahmad, he was surprised that the CPRF had acted so quickly. He told Ahmad to watch his back and lay low, where he was until he could get back to him.

After placing a call to the ruling committee in Tehran, he told them of the Russian action.

The realization that the Russians had learned about the incident planning, including the Iranian participation, meant that they longer needed to involve them. Iran didn't need the three highly placed Russian committee members any longer. They were out of reach anyway, and the CPRF would most likely take care of them. They instructed Naseem to see if he could have the Russian Captain and his mate removed and silenced, then recall his cousin to Azerbaijan.

Back in Volgograd, Ahmad had listened to his cousin's instructions and thought about how he could make all this happen.

There was a way, although a bit risky.

After calling Ziolkowski and Heilig on the phone and telling them that he had been instructed, for their safety, to get them to Derbent by train tomorrow, once there, arrangements were being set up for them to travel to Baku.

He then began to lay out his plan.

He would get tickets for himself, Ziolkowski, and Heilig to board a train bound for Derbent, tomorrow morning. He thought that he could arrange it so that a bomb would detonate as they cleared the city limits and entered into the dense forest southeast of the city.

The rest of that evening, he used his skill to create a firebomb that, when ignited, would cause a fireball of about twenty feet in diameter. Adding the finished bomb to his suitcase, he would have it, hidden under clothes, with him as they all boarded the train the next morning.

He reserved a private cabin for the three of them, and it went as he had planned. When they all got aboard, he placed his suitcase on the overhead rack next to both Ziolkowski's and Heilig's bags.

As the train was ready to pull out of the station, he waited for the usual sudden start, and when it occurred, it allowed him to spill his coffee. With a hot wet stain on his pants, he got up to go to the toilet and clean himself off.

Standing by the exit door next to the toilet, he heard a sudden 'whoosh' of an explosion, and a large ball of fire blasted out of their cabin door.

Of course, there was an immediate fire alarm going off, and the train pulled to a quick stop.

In the ensuing panic, Ahmad jumped off the train and ran into the woods. He joined the growing number of panicking passengers running from the train.

As many of those passengers made it out to the main road, police and fire rescue trucks arrived.

The train was only a mile from the edge of town, and Ahmad just walked along with the ever-expanding crowd as they entered the streets and began to disperse.

Back aboard the train, the fire crews could put out the fire and begin a search of the remains of the two charred bodies still in their seats, looking for identification.

That evening, Ahmad, was already on a flight to Azerbaijan. He was landing at the international airport in Baku when notification of the two dead bodies' positive identities, from the train, reached both Victor Polanski at Russian Naval Operations and the CPRF president's desk in Moscow.

Since there was no report from the KGB, they now knew that there was someone else involved. With that, it was time for a belated investigation into the three Committee members; it could no longer wait.

CHAPTER TWENTY-EIGHT

Monday, 22 April 2019
NSIU Headquarters
Washington D.C.

Connie was still a bit tired when she got to work Monday morning. She had a very busy weekend, moving into a new place.

After transferring to NSIU and spending almost a month looking for a place to stay, she found a brand-new townhouse. It is just outside the beltway, on the northwest side of Washington.

It is about thirteen hundred square feet and is the new open concept style, with the kitchen, living space, and dining area all in one large open room. There are two bedrooms upstairs, two baths, and an attached one-car garage.

It was only a ten-minute drive to NSIU headquarters, yet far enough away from the busy town's center, so she was in a country-style neighborhood. She had been lucky to find it so fast, as they were selling like hotcakes.

She hadn't been sure that she wanted to buy a place, since she had always rented before. But it was all finished, ready to go, and the deal was just too good to pass up.

Saturday morning, a moving truck arrived a little after nine o'clock in the morning. It was loaded with all her stuff that they had cleared out of her storage unit the day before. She barely beat them to the house, about five minutes before they arrived.

As she showed the movers around, Paul, Ira, Antonio, Luigi, and Linda arrived together, surprising her, and dressed in work clothes ready to help her get things set up and going.

Connie couldn't help herself; tears of joy and appreciation clouded her eyes at the realization that the people at NSIU really cared about her as a friend.

Although it took most of the weekend, she finally got everything put away. She was insistent that her friends were to stay for a Sunday afternoon meal. She wanted to prepare it for them, trying out her new stove while they all watched a golf tournament on television.

Admiral Walker arrived a few minutes after Connie got to work, and stopped at her office to ask if all went well and tell her that he was pleased she was settled.

At the Ten o'clock Monday briefing in the third-floor conference room, light chatter was going around the table when Harold came in and sat next to Connie. He had a strange look on his face. And as she turned to ask him what was wrong, he said, shaking his head: "I got a call at home from the CIA, and ten minutes later from Nigel, in London."

Then with a smile, added: "Let's hold off for a few minutes, and we can all hear about everything without having to repeat it."

Admiral Walker came in and sat down, holding the files from his lockbox in his hand.

The Monday briefing usually followed a normal procedure of first reading the items in the lockbox from DOD, followed by investigation updates, and then the assignments were handed out.

Today, however, the Admiral also saw the strange look on Harold's face and changed the procedure.

"Harold," he said, "something is bothering you, and we all notice it, so what has happened?"

Harold, shaking his head and laughing, said: "You all know me too well. Yes, something has happened.

"I was awakened at three-thirty this morning with a coded call from a CIA agent we have in Moscow. It was a short report, and it said that

CPRF Committee Advisor, Boris Kanski, had gone down to Volgograd to probably escape from issues regarding his participation in the Sub incident. Before he met with anyone there, two KGB agents took him out with a poisoned needle.

"The next morning, that would be last Friday, the Sub's Captain and his second in command were on a train bound for Derbent when a fireball erupted in their cabin, killing them both. A third person was registered in that cabin, but he wasn't in it when it exploded.

"That third person was Ahmad Abd-El-Kader, from Yemen."

"No, that can't be!" Said Ira, "How did he get to Volgograd?"

Harold answered: "Well, Ira, the CIA isn't our only source of information; I also got a call from Nigel at MI-5 this morning. I had told him about the likely Iranian connection, with the UAE tank sabotage, last week when he first called, and he added that name to their travel watch list.

"He told me the same information that I got from the CIA, but the Brits have a good network in Russia as well. Also, because of the EU's free travel policy, they have developed a link into many computers that record flight or train travel, departures, and arrivals. It lists passengers traveling into and out of any country with connections to the U.K. and the EU.

Ironically, that includes many Eastern European and Middle Eastern countries as well.

"Nigel told me that he had plugged in Ahmad Abd-El-Kader's name and information, and it popped right up. He got a list of his travels for the last week."

Looking down at his notes, he continued: "He left Yemen on 11 April with a flight to Volgograd, changing planes in Tehran. The next listing was for the 19 April, ill-fated train connection to Derbent. He moved fast, because he was on that train in the morning and then on a Flight that same afternoon from Volgograd to Baku, Azerbaijan. We believe he is currently there."

Paul spoke up at that point: "It would seem that he is an expert with explosives and various means of destruction. It also seems likely that he has no qualms about killing people."

"It would seem so!" Said Ira: "But when we traced him in the UAE, the report from Saudi Arabia did mention that his only known living relative was a cousin who is an Islamic Cleric in Baku, Azerbaijan."

Then looking through his notes, continued: "His name is Naseem Sargon, and, although unconfirmed, the only information we have, about him, is that he is believed to have direct connections with the Islamic leadership in Tehran."

Connie had been listening carefully, and things started to click in her head. She looked up and asked: "If that is true, then is the UAE tank episode an Iranian fronted sabotage?"

Harold answered: "It looks that way. Why?"

Connie answered: "If so, then the attack was likely intended to cause embarrassment to the Emirates by disrupting their fuel containment policy. It wouldn't be a big loss, but the embarrassment would still be there.

Although Rudy sat quietly listening to the revelation and the ensuing discussion, his mind kept going to Azerbaijan's actual history and the connections that had never really changed.

Although part of the ancient Persian territory, Azerbaijan was politically pulled back and forth between Russia and Iran for centuries. It had been incorporated into the Soviet Union for two-thirds of the twentieth century until its break up in 1991. But, despite its new independence, it still has strong ties to both its neighbors.

Rudy wondered which side was pulling the strings on this overall situation, Russia or Iran?

He smiled to himself, slightly shook his head, and let out a short little laugh.

Linda, who was sitting next to him, looked over and asked: "What are you thinking about Rudy?"

He answered: "I just thought that there always seems to be a strange conflict of actions between the Russians and the Iranians. That could be explained with the actual history in that part of the world, except what we have learned so far, is the universal target from both of them is us, here in the United States."

Connie said: "That is what I meant by they seem intended to cause embarrassment to the Emirates, and us, and, perhaps even to several of the other oil-producing countries; that would effectively result in a decrease in the available product, reducing competition."

Paul said: "Yes, Connie, I agree. However, I think that it may even be more than just targeting the oil-rich countries, including us. I think they are in the middle of a power struggle in Russia, and Iran is simply taking advantage of the situation.

"After all, three Russians were killed last week, and all three, we suspect of being involved with the Sub incident.

"What seems to indicate a power struggle is a fact that Kanski, who was in the CPRF, was killed by the KGB, who are Russian. Where the two Russian Naval officers were, we think, killed by Abd-El-Kader, who, at least, appears to be under Iranian influence."

The admiral said: "These are all very good points, but if it is true, there is little we can do about it."

CHAPTER TWENTY-NINE

Monday, 22 April 2019
Communist Party of the Russian Federation (CPRF)
Office of the President
Moscow, Russia

The president was sitting at his desk reading the intelligence report he had received that morning when a knock on the door announced the arrival of the head of security, Ivan Gorg. He was also the head of the KGB.

After telling him to come in, he asked: "Have you determined who Kanski was reporting to yet?"

Without saying anything, Gorg handed him three files that had been secured with sealing wax.

As the president took the files, broke the seals, and slowly withdrew the single sheet of paper from each one. His expression never changed as he read the names and looked at the pictures. He looked up at Gorg and asked: "Are you absolutely sure?"

Gorg answered: "Yes sir, we have multiple written and taped copies of communications between them, and also with Kanski, all containing details of actions regarding their attempt to take over control of the Party.

"We have not moved in on them, and I believe they are unaware of our depth of knowledge. However, when Kanski went down to Volgograd, they may have been alarmed that their plot was starting to unravel. I had our agents there quickly find him and have him neutralized."

The president said: "I have this report from Naval operations that both Captain Ziolkowski and Captain 3rd Heilig were also taken out. The report says that they were kept in a place where they could be watched, but somehow, they decided to get out, only to be killed. Who did it?"

Gorg said: "The report we got, from our agents in Volgograd, was that a firebomb was placed in their compartment on the express train to Derbent. We believe it was placed by the third person traveling with them. However, he wasn't in the compartment when it went off, just as the train left the city.

"We have an identification of that man, his name is Ahmad Abd-El-Kader, from Yemen. We have not found him yet, but his connections, we believe, are in Azerbaijan.

He is a strong Islamic, as were Ziolkowski and Heilig, and after checking travel records, he was on a flight that same evening from Volgograd to Baku.

With his hands folded on his desk and without a change in expression, the president looked at the man in front of him, then picking up the three files and waving them at Gorg, said: "These three men had a plan that we believe is now ended. Their actions, however, cost us a nuclear submarine and worldwide embarrassment. I think we need to have something happen that will stop any future attempts like this to occur. An example must be made of them."

"Yes sir," said Gorg: "How much of an example. I am sure you know that they do have friends and associates in powerful places."

"I understand that," said the president, "so, let us publicly indicate that we are conducting a research project about the radioactive contamination sickness that nearly killed our sailors aboard the Nikolayevich Kosinski."

Then with a smile, said: "We will have them volunteer to do this research themselves, from inside the barrier zone at Chernobyl, and make sure they each become contaminated. That way, they will suffer a great deal of agony, yet it will let them die as heroes."

Later that same day, the president met with the Navel director, Victor Polanski, to ask him about planned training operations in the Caspian Sea.

He wanted to have a strong showing of naval power all along the coast of Iran; this was to signal to their leaders in Tehran that the Russians were a far more advanced and superior power.

At the same time, he would also have the Russian Air Force do practice close combat air maneuvers along the edge of, and into, Iranian air space.

These actions were meant to send a clear message to the Iranian leadership. It would leave no doubt that Russia knew what had happened. It would also let them know that Iran has stepped over a line with their support of the attempted coup d'état, and any continued actions would have very severe consequences.

CHAPTER THIRTY

Tuesday, 23 April 2019
NSIU Headquarters
Washington D.C.

Harold, Linda, Connie, and Paul were sitting in Harold's office, talking about the revelations around them. None of them had ever had an experience like this before. It had them each wondering exactly what had occurred that made these questions so difficult. No, they knew what had occurred; they just didn't know what they should be doing about it.

Connie, who was the least experienced with this type of investigation, but having spent seven years teaching, said: "I wonder, if maybe we each took some time and wrote down a list of all that has happened, then compared them; we might find an answer as to what, if anything, we need to do next."

Harold looked over at her and said: "Connie, that has been a practice many of us have used frequently. But this time, I think you have just stated the best procedure we can have. Usually, it is just Paul or me who prepares an outline, but this one is too confusing. So, I propose that we take Connie's suggestion and have all of us, who have any thoughts, regardless of how remote from the incident it may seem to be, prepare, in outline form, what we know or have learned."

Linda, drawing on her experience from law enforcement, said: "Yes, that is a good idea; however, this time, Nigel Donaldson at MI-5 has become just as involved. Is it proper for us to ask if he would also participate in this outline? Perhaps, even coming here to Washington or you, Harold, maybe going over to London?"

Paul had been quiet and just sat there half-listening to the others. As the conversation slowed a bit, he said: "Our original order, from DOD, was to look into the cause of the Russian Submarine Incident and try to determine exactly how and why it occurred, and who was responsible.

"Not to belittle the point, we have done that; and could submit our findings in a report now.

"Unfortunately, each of us is far more curious than we are supposed to be, and thus we just keep digging.

"That isn't bad, or wrong, or anything else, but it does sometimes take us up a different trail. I think that this is the case here.

"So, I propose the following: We write the report to DOD for the original Submarine incident. Please submit it to DOD and closeout that part of the case.

"Then let's open a new question, an advisory question, that we follow all the trails we have so far determined. We then submit either a collective outline or perhaps an opinion report of everything else we have discovered. That report should go to both DOD and DOS for them to decide what, if anything, must be done."

Harold said: "That sounds like a sound strategy Paul, let me run it by the admiral, and maybe make a few phone calls, and we can meet again this afternoon.

The admiral agreed to the overall suggestion. He then told Harold that although the NSIU had answered the DOD inquiry, it must inform them, the DOS, and even the DOJ, that all of us feel a responsibility to investigate it further because of the implications found.

Harold's phone call to Nigel in London ended with an agreement that Harold would fly over to London, and the two of them could get together and share a joint outline of the Russian and Iranian positions.

Over the next two days, Harold took his time writing the report to DOD about the Incident itself, while Paul, Linda, Connie, Ira, Antonio, Luigi, and Rudy each looked through their notes and listed all the items and opinions they had discovered.

It was a difficult task because there was no specific crime or action that they were looking at, and for the first time in their experiences, they each felt there was something more to come. The United States had not been physically attacked, and there was no case of any destruction of American property; to the contrary, America was seen worldwide as a paragon of goodwill and concern for saving the Russian sailors and securing the safe disposal of the problem.

Thursday afternoon, there was a meeting in the third-floor conference room with everyone except Harold. He was on an afternoon flight to meet with Nigel at MI-5 in London tomorrow morning.

It was decided that Connie would be the one to write an outline of items that would include as much of the input from everyone as possible. Of course, there was much duplication of items, but each time there would be an opinion that could move it differently.

The items and thoughts they could list were based on the following:

1. The items listed in the incident report to DOD, that Harold had written, included:

a.) The Radioactive leak was caused by an explosive charge placed on the top of the reactor cover.

b.) It was a planned explosion, set up and done by the Submarine senior crew, i.e., the Captain and his second in command.

c.) It actually was a hoax, intended to create a simulated attack on the United States crude oil supply. The hoax was to cause an environmental disaster that would place worldwide condemnation on America. However, this incident's real intention was to cause significant embarrassment to the Russian government, particularly to the CPRF president.

d.) The actual orders for the incident originated with several senior members of the CPRF, believed to be planning a coup d'état, using connections with the Islamic community in Russia, but accessed, through side agreements, with the Iranian leadership from Tehran, Iran.

2. Items that cause concerns that were found but not specifically connected to the Submarine incident include:

a.) It was determined that the course of the Submarine, if it had been allowed to follow its original orders, was to create an oil spill somewhere near the Bay of Valdez.

b.) It would indicate that the Russians were trying to create an environmental embarrassment; one that would force the Americans to cut back on their oil production. The Submarine was to be well remote from the area before detonation of an explosive mine attached to oil barrels it had left in that area.

c.) A meeting between a North Sea Oil company executive, Christopher Bing, and the Iranian attaché to Switzerland, Darvish Abthai, revealed a connection between the aid, Boris Kanski, for the CPRF conspirators, and the Iranians.

d.) A fuel oil tank explosion in the UAE involving unusual circumstances, showed it was sabotage and identified the individual who did it. It was determined that he was an individual from Yemen, named Ahmad Abd-El-Kader, with connections to an Islamic cleric, named Naseem Sargon, in Azerbaijan, who has strong ties and connections to Iran.

e.) From a discussion with four unconnected business executives in New York City, it was explained that the United States' shift to energy independence, along with its increased production of crude oil, had reduced America's need to import foreign oil. This shift caused a change in the global competition for supply, thus creating a significant drop in future trade values. Those changes in the oil futures value make the American supply chain a target for anyone who wanted to regain the former uncontested marketplace. The target those executives indicated, as the most probable, is the offshore drilling platforms that follow the coastline of the Gulf of Mexico from Galveston, Texas, to Mobile, Alabama.

f.) Recent activity, discovered in Russia, by the CIA, and confirmed by MI-5, showed a coup d'état conspiracy had likely been discovered. The conspirator's aid, Boris Kanski, attempting to escape, was found and assassinated by the KGB in Volgograd.

g.) The following morning, Captain Ziolkowski and his second in command, Captain 3rd Heilig, from the Submarine, were killed by a firebomb. It had been planted in their compartment on a train while they were attempting escape from Volgograd. It was discovered that the bomb was created and placed by the same man from Yemen, Ahmad Abd-El-Kader, now believed to be in Baku, Azerbaijan.

h.) Recent activity in Tehran, and throughout Iran, with citizen demonstrations and riots, has had the effect of weakening the Iranian leadership. It was noted that the increase in oil competition has strongly decreased Iran's economy.

As Connie finished entering all the points on her laptop, she looked up at the others in the room and asked: "There is a lot of information here, and yet I think we have only touched the surface; what else can we add at this time?

Linda answered: "We can expound on each of these items, but it will always come back to just what we have stated."

Paul spoke up: "If I was to summarize this, I would simply state that Iran, although behind these actions, is in trouble; and looking for some way to reinstate control over their people.

"All roads keep coming back to them, and they seem to have associated themselves with certain partners who either agree with their program or are using it to gain their own ends."

CHAPTER THIRTY-ONE

Friday, 26 April 2019
MI-5 Offices of Investigation
London, UK

Harold had arrived at London's Gatwick Airport very early Friday morning. He was planning on taking the train connection from the airport to the ExCel London station and then a short taxi ride to the Hilton hotel, before he would call Nigel.

At least, that is what he had planned to do, but as he was walking down the off-ramp from the arrival terminal, a tall, strong London Bobbie placed himself right in Harold's face and said: "And just where do you think you are going, Yankee?"

Harold, who hadn't slept on the flight and was a bit tired, looked at the big constable blocking his way, and the thought in his head was: 'What the hell is this all about?' when a friendly voice behind him said: "It's alright officer, you don't need to cuff him, I'll just take him, downtown with me."

Harold turned around and looked at a smiling Nigel Donaldson standing right behind him, who said: "You told me you were coming, did you think I wouldn't find out how and when, so I could come and get you, after all this time?"

Harold, with a big smile on his face, said: "Nigel, you dog, you better remember that I never get mad, but I always get even!" Then turning with a smile to the Bobbie, he said: "I suppose I should be mad at you, but I know this crazy guy just set you up, so I'll just say thank you and have a nice day." With that, the Bobbie touched his helmet with his nightstick and said: "Welcome to London, sir; enjoy your stay."

As they walked over to Nigel's car, Harold noticed that a driver was standing by the door waiting for them. He looked at Nigel and said: "They don't let you drive anymore? I can't say I blame them; you always had a strange idea on which side of the road to drive on."

Nigel gave him a dirty look and said: "Just get in, or I'll take you back and give you to that big Bobbie back there."

As they settled in the back-seat, Nigel handed Harold a hot to-go cup, saying: "No complaints, I had to find a place that actually had that terrible coffee you drink, and they all laughed at me when I ordered it."

The two friends continued insulting each other until they crossed into London proper. Although Harold figured the driver was from MI-5, he refrained from asking Nigel anything about the investigation. It wasn't high security, but it was standard procedure to be sure.

About half an hour later, they were both sitting in Nigel's office, going over the files that they had obtained from MI-5's field service agents in both Russia and Iran. Harold had forwarded the CIA intelligence reports, over a secure transmission, with the information about the Russian activities, and as they compared them, found they were remarkably similar. The information regarding Iran was more detailed than the American files. The UK had some relations with them, albeit not much better, but they did have up to date and better access to the European Union intelligence reports.

Nigel said: "I don't know if a meeting with Christopher Bing would gain us anything, but we can take a short flight up to Aberdeen and talk to him; he wants to help, and I believe he is concerned about the Iran proposal. He has not answered any request from Iran attaché Abthai in Switzerland, as yet; he is waiting for us to tell him what he should do.

"He hasn't mentioned it, but I think that he is concerned about his drilling platforms in the North Sea. When he finally drops the proposal, they may become a target for a sabotage attempt. It is a real possibility."

Harold said: "You are right, it is a possibility, and it wouldn't be too difficult for one of Iran's agents to get to it. I know that there are quite a few of those platforms up there, and access wouldn't be too difficult."

"No" said Nigel, "it wouldn't be difficult; although the countries surrounding that sea area aren't largely involved with the drilling process, they still help us provide a good security watch over those drilling rigs. However, there are a lot of places that a small sabotage attempt could attack from. It is a concern."

Harold said: "Have you found anything further about the man from Yemen, Ahmad Abd-El-Kader? Is he still in Azerbaijan?"

Nigel picked up his phone and called someone in their research department and asked about him. After listening for a moment, he hung up the phone, turned to his computer screen, and punched in a number.

"I should have been more alert," he said, "he flew from Baku to St. Petersburg yesterday. I am surprised that the Russians haven't jumped all over him yet. But having him in St. Petersburg puts him in a position of access to the Baltic Sea, and a clear shot, for a small, fast boat, to the North Sea."

Harold said: "Maybe it is a good idea for us to go see Mr. Bing up in Aberdeen. If he has turned down the Iranian proposal, then his company could become an easy target, and that could also cause an environmental issue; if a leak or spill is generated."

"I think you may well be right," said Nigel, "are you up for a couple of hour flight to Scotland?"

At two-thirty that afternoon, Harold and Nigel were shown into Bing's office in Aberdeen. Bing was nervous at first when they arrived but quickly gained his calm back when they told him that they were concerned that his refusal of attaché Abtahi's proposal might be an opening for them to plan a sabotage attempt on one of his rigs.

Bing said: "The North Sea platforms are made for rough weather, and it would take a great deal of effort even to make any type of an attack to sabotage one of them."

He told them that most of the private companies had realized long ago that all of their existence depended upon each other for surveillance and survival.

He then took both of them down to his monitoring headquarters in the basement. One wall, about thirty-five feet long and eighteen feet high, was covered with huge television screens. The pictures on those screens were from hundreds of security cameras located on over forty-eight supply and drilling platforms.

Bing introduced his head security officer to Harold and Nigel, and he explained the depth of security that was mounted on each rig. They watched carefully, looking for anything unusual; the cameras had special motion detection, and recordings are kept for thirty days from each camera. They had twelve people who continuously monitored the screens around the clock.

Ironically, it wasn't sabotage they were worried about, but severe weather and high seas were their biggest concerns. However, if there was an attempt of sabotage, they had a helicopter response security force that could be on any of the platforms within twenty minutes of an alarm.

With the knowledge that Ahmad Abd-El-Kader was in St. Petersburg, it could likely mean that the Iranians had figured that the silence from Deep Ice Oil company meant Bing would refuse the proposal made by attaché Abthai. He was, therefore, in place to create a spill at one of their rigs.

Harold and Nigel, along with Christopher Bing, sat and put together a plan. With Bing's agreement, MI-5 would assign a platoon of special forces Rangers, who would temporally replace Bing's security force. They would also provide additional surveillance of the oil platforms, including high altitude flight monitoring of craft approaching the area. They would have everything in place by Sunday evening.

Bing was then instructed to officially decline the Iranian proposal. It was done in the form of a fax sent to attaché Abthai that afternoon.

CHAPTER THIRTY-TWO

Saturday, 27 April 2019
Shinseki Hotel
St. Petersburg, Russia

Ahmad Abd-El-Kader was in St. Petersburg. He had been ready to return to his home in Yemen when he was summoned by his cousin Naseem Sargon to do another job for the Tehran leaders. They hadn't heard anything from Christopher Bing concerning their proposal to ally with Bing's company, 'Deep Ice Oil.'

That proposal was made to Bing to let Iran get out of their alliance agreement with Russia for those lucrative E.U. fuel oil contracts.

They assumed that he was declining the proposal, and therefore his company became available as a target for sabotage to reduce competition. Ahmad was told to do something that would create an embarrassment for the U.K.'s oil production in the North Sea and punish Bing at the same time.

He thought about it, and it seemed that the simple way was to knock two of the legs off one of their production platforms and let gravity take it down the rest of the way. Along with a broken oil line, at sea level, it would result in a large spill and 'oil slick' on the surface of the sea.

He hadn't been sure just how he could get to the oil field area, but Naseem had connections with a fair-sized group of dissidents in St. Petersburg.

Those people were supporters of the attempted Coup d'état that was supposed to happen in Moscow, yet now it seemed to be failing, after the death of Boris Kanski was reported.

After being advised of Abd-El-Kader's mission, the group's leader met him when he arrived in St. Petersburg Friday night and arranged space for him at a small hotel on the East side of town, near the private shipping piers that were on the Gulf of Finland.

This group of dissidents, although relatively small, was made up of a mix of working-class people, small business owners, and some transplanted people from Western Europe.

They owned and operated a small eight container transport delivery freighter, named 'Boxxer'. It was known to make weekly freight runs both to and from St. Petersburg, across the Baltic Sea with stops in Helsinki, Finland, Stockholm, Sweden, Copenhagen, Denmark, and then across the North Sea to Aberdeen, Scotland.

Their cargo was almost always agricultural, in both directions, so the customs inspections were very slight or, sometimes even non-existent, as they entered or left the various ports.

The next trip was scheduled to leave on Sunday morning, with arrival at their final destination of Aberdeen late Tuesday evening.

This arrangement was perfect for Abd-El-Kader's mission; he could place a small inflatable boat in one of the containers, and, as it would pass near the oil platforms by Aberdeen, they could launch him in the small boat. He could then, using his GPS, locate the nearest 'Deep Ice Oil' platform, and place his explosive charges where they would do the most damage. He would have all night to get the charges in position and then, using a GPS, return to be picked up the next morning soon after first light. He could then wait until they were at least twenty miles away from the platforms before he remotely set them off.

The program was well thought out, and he spent Saturday putting together the explosive charges he would need. The North Sea area, where the platforms are located, was relatively narrow between Scotland and Denmark, about five-hundred nautical miles, and with the oil platforms used as cell towers, mobile phone signals were strong and reliable almost everywhere.

His calculation involved three separate explosive charges, but they needed to be independent of each other because they would be too far apart to connect by wire. So, he purchased three separate cell phones and rigged them to close the ignition circuit on the explosives individually when he dialed their numbers. The last thing he needed to do as he left the charges in place was to turn on those cell phones.

The crew of the 'Boxxer' found a gray inflatable boat with a forty horse-power outboard motor and a 'Bimini' top to keep him out of the weather. They stocked it with the tools he would need to secure the charges to the platform, and enough food and water supplies to last him all night.

At ten o'clock Sunday morning with all items in place, including Abd-El-Kader hiding inside one of the containers with his boat and explosives, the 'Boxxer' left port on the first leg of its normal weekly trip. Once they were out on open water, Abd-El-Kader was let out and could enjoy the cruse. But the crew was known, at each port, so he needed to hide in the container at every port. However, the risk of discovery was low, so he had no complaint.

CHAPTER THIRTY-THREE

Tuesday, 30 April 2019
'Deep Ice Oil Company' Headquarters
Aberdeen, Scotland

MI-5 could act fast when they needed to, and when they realized they were setting up a possible trap to prevent a disastrous environmental attack, they were very capable.

Nigel and Harold spent the weekend up in Scotland, both taking a little time off to play some golf on the 'Old Course' at Saint Andrews.

Nigel called his wife to tell her he was staying there for the weekend; and that he had a rare opportunity to beat a 'Yankee' in the ancient game, at the birthplace of golf, proving to him that the British are still better at most things.

Elaine, his wife, laughing said: "Nigel, you know very well that you have wanted to play up there for years, and I find it a rare and delightful opportunity to see you get your butt kicked by an American. Please give my very best to Harold, and try to bring him back here for dinner before he heads back to America.

Out on the course, it became obvious that the two special agents, from their respective countries, were much better security men than golfers, but they had a lot of fun playing and harassing each other.

By Monday noon, there were eleven British Army rangers and three attack helicopters ready and waiting in the Aberdeen area. Most of them stayed at the Gordon Barracks and could directly access the security camera connections, and they worked closely with the company's staff watching them.

Like the Americans, the British air force always has several aircraft in the air twenty-four hours a day, seven days a week; and they are equipped to monitor pretty much anything that goes on around the U.K. at any time.

Harold had been in contact with a CIA asset in St. Petersburg, who found Abd-El-Kader and reported that he was staying with a group of Russian dissidents believed to have connections with Iran.

Nigel took that information and passed it through the MI-5 agents in Russia. He learned that the members of that particular group were a mix of people, known to have been a thorn in the side of the CDRF for years. It was also known that many of them were indirectly connected to the Islamic leaders in Iran.

Interestingly enough, it was also known that they operated a small container shipping company. It serviced an agricultural trade business between their nearby neighboring countries, including Scotland, in the U.K. They had only one small, two-hundred-foot-long flat top freighter, named 'Boxxer,' with its port of call in St. Petersburg. It made a weekly round trip delivery run amongst those various country's ports.

As MI-5 in London looked into the normal shipping schedule of the 'Boxxer,' they found it usually arrived in Aberdeen about eight o'clock on Tuesday evening. It would unload three containers, and take on three new containers bound for the various ports on their route back to St. Petersburg. They would spend the rest of the night at the port in Aberdeen, leaving just before dawn on Wednesday morning for the return three-day trip, and arriving in St. Petersburg about eight o'clock on Friday evening.

Security traced their normal course, across the North Sea, showing that late in the afternoon, they would pass about twelve miles south of the oil drilling and support platforms that were in service from the Aberdeen Area.

In St. Petersburg, the 'Boxxer,' with Abd-El-Kader hidden inside the rearmost container, left port at ten o'clock Sunday morning. After clearing into open water, Abd-El-Kader was able to come out of the container and enjoy the open sea's fresh air. He would repeat this action of hiding as they stopped at each port.

Because the longest leg of the trip was from Copenhagen to Aberdeen, about five hundred nautical miles and would take about sixteen hours, the 'Boxxer' would leave Denmark at midnight. That would put it about twelve miles south of the target drilling platform just about five o'clock in the afternoon. Once the ship cleared port in Copenhagen and made the turn onto the North Sea, there was little else he could do, so he spent the time sleeping and checking his equipment.

At four-forty-five, Tuesday afternoon, everything was ready. As the ship slowed to a stop, Abd-El-Kader and his inflatable was launched. Five minutes later, he had started his outboard and pulled away from the now moving again 'Boxxer.'

The weather had been his only concern, and it had worked in his favor; the seas were relatively calm, and there was a low cloud cover over most of the area. By seven-thirty, he could see the platform, just off to his right side. The sun had already set, but there was enough light for him to begin his approach.

He had planned to make sure no one saw him there, and the total quiet around the platform indicated that he had figured it well. He had calculated that it would take him about two hours to move to the locations where he could set up the three explosive charges. It would still give him plenty of time to return to his GPS pick up location.

He had figured that since he wasn't going to ignite the explosions until he was back aboard the 'Boxxer,' there was little or no danger of anyone finding him.

Back ashore, the U.K. Army rangers were waiting for something to happen when a high-altitude air force resonance plane picked up on radar the 'Boxxer.' It was right on its intended route. Still, it had then slowed to a stop, then five minutes later, had accelerated back to its cruising speed.

That was enough for one of the attack helicopters to take off and fly to the 'Deep Ice Oil' platform. It was the one that MI-5 calculated was the target. It only took twenty-five minutes, and when the team of Rangers landed on the platform, they quickly moved to camouflage the helicopter with a cover.

It was only about an hour-and-a-half later, the team on the platform was called. They were told that security cameras and motion detectors had picked up a target several hundred yards south of the rig.

The Army Rangers had planned to watch the terrorist begin to place his explosives, and then they would move in on him before he could detonate them. Six Rangers were situated on the edge of the platform, waiting for him to arrive. Once he was under it, they would drop ropes and quickly belay down with weapons drawn and aimed at him.

As they were in position, two of them saw Abd-El-Kader and his camouflaged inflatable boat gently rocking as it slowly moved under the rig. With a click in each of their earpieces, all six executed their drill with precision. As they dropped down, Abd-El-Kader was almost directly in the middle of the rig. He then heard the Ranger commander's call for him to stop and place his hands on his head.

He was many things, immoral, and without care, but he wasn't stupid. He looked up at the guns, pointing at him, and followed instructions. Three of the Rangers were dive equipped, entered the water, swam to the inflatable where they climbed aboard, cuffed him, and pulled the boat out into the clear night air. Within the next ten minutes, the helicopter loaded with all remaining equipment on the deck had picked up the rangers from the water, loaded their prisoner, diffused the explosives, and hooked a line that would carry the inflatable back to Aberdeen.

The British Army, with direction from MI-5, loaded the inflatable on the helicopter and flew it to the same location, at sea, where the 'Boxxer' had stopped the previous afternoon.

At eight-forty-five, the 'Boxxer' stopped at the same point to pick up Abd-El-Kader's inflatable, only to find it was empty.

At almost the same time, a U.K. Army helicopter showed up just above the stopped ship. With weapons pointed at it, there was no question that they were not to move. A radio call from the Helicopter confirmed that, and said that a U.K. Navy cruiser would shortly pull alongside and they would be detained.

CHAPTER THIRTY-FOUR

Monday, 6 May 2019
NSIU Headquarters
Washington D.C.

Early Monday morning, Connie had arrived before almost everyone else, except for both Seaman Jimmy Louis and Seaman Susan Gordon. Those two always tried to be the first to arrive at NSIU every weekday morning, so they could check with the nighttime security guards and navy watch staff for any general messages that they needed to document before everyone else arrived.

She was getting more and more comfortable with her new house, located outside the Washington beltway, and in the early morning, before eight o'clock, there was very little traffic where she was.

This morning, it was Seaman Jimmy Louis who handed her a message as she arrived. It was from the Admiral, and it asked her to please be in uniform today, as there was likely to be a special meeting over at DOS, and he would like her to go with him.

She had been assigned to NSIU for just over a month and realized that, although they dressed in civilian attire most of the time, everyone always kept their uniforms there just in case. The calendar had tripped into May, and she had, fortunately, remembered to bring her 'dress whites' in with her this morning.

She had no sooner walked to the break room to turn on the coffee pot when Harold came in right behind her. As they both waited for the pot to heat up, she asked him how his flight was and when he got in?

Harold said: "I got in Saturday afternoon. I was able to catch a non-stop flight out of Gatwick at nine o'clock Saturday morning.

"It was Nigel's wife Elaine, who refused to take 'I need to go home,' for an answer; and insisted on preparing a really fine dinner for us on Friday night, when we got back from Scotland. She is very sweet and a bloody great chef. She prepared a dinner of beef Wellington with boiled potatoes and carrots, with apple cobbler and ice cream for dessert. The three of us together then polished off a bottle of Côte du Rhône Beaujolais; that was the crown on the evening's meal.

"I don't know how Nigel stays so thin! But it was worth waiting another day to come home."

As they got their coffee, Harold asked: "Has there been any comments about the MI-5 and U.K. Army actions yet."

Connie answered: "It was kind of like a big sigh of relief; when we heard that the bomber was captured. I am sure there will be many questions about it at this morning's meeting."

Two minutes before ten o'clock, Connie, in her 'dress whites,' entered the conference room. She was surprised to notice that everyone else was also in their dress white uniforms, and they all were sitting at the conference table, just normally chatting before the ten o'clock meeting.

Admiral Walker, also in his dress white uniform, entered the room, smiled at everyone, and said before sitting down: "Before we start our meeting today, I have someone I would like to introduce to all of you. With that, Chief Petty Officer Paul DeNice quickly stood to attention and said sharply: "Attention!"

As everyone rose and stood at attention, Billy Wicks, also in his dress whites, entered the room. He smiled at everyone, and particularly at Lieutenant Commander Connie Wall.

Admiral Walker said: "I'd like to introduce Rear-Admiral Billy Wicks of the United States Coast Guard." Turning toward Billy, he said, nodding: "Admiral."

Rear-Admiral Billy Wicks said: "At ease; it is a pleasure to meet and see all of you. And with a nod to Admiral Walker, said: "Thank you, Admiral, for allowing me this opportunity."

Then turning to Connie, said: "Lieutenant Commander Connie Wall; please forgive us for this surprise. But this was in the works for several months, well before you were transferred to the NSIU Command. It is something that a number of your fellow officers, in New London, and I thought should have happened a while ago.

Then walking over to stand in front of Connie, said: "It is my pleasure, and a very great honor, to award you the promotion to the rank of a Full Line Commander in the United States Coast Guard."

Then giving her the new shoulder boards of a Commander, with the three full stripes, to replace the existing two and a half stripes of a Lieutenant Commander, shook her hand then, standing back and straight, they saluted each other; the whole room exploded in applause."

Connie was shocked and didn't know what to say. But, as a former instructor at the Coast Guard OCS, she knew to remain stiff at attention and follow all the etiquette rules, but that was automatic; she was completely surprised.

The ten o'clock meeting was over at that point, at least as a meeting. It had turned into a celebration event to honor Connie's advancement, and everyone wanted to congratulate her and wish her continued success. When things had calmed down a little, Linda, the only civilian there, congratulated Connie and told her how pleased she was. Connie took the opportunity to tell Linda that it was the friendship of all the people at NSIU that made everything so very special.

On Tuesday morning, things started to get back to normal.

Admiral Wicks, after spending all the previous day at NSIU, then providing a banquet at the French Bistro, on Iowa street, for the whole NSIU team, had gone back to New London, Connecticut.

Connie, back in Civilian clothes today, was still a bit in shock about the whole thing.

As the ten o'clock meeting began, Admiral Walker started it off by asking Harold to please go over the lockbox's normal requests.

There was little new in it this week, except DOD's question if there was anything different from what had been included in the Russian Submarine incident.

Then glancing over at Paul, he decided to refrain from telling everyone that Chicago, once again had a question about their weekly crime situation.

He then said: "Following Paul's suggestion, we sent this response to the DOD regarding their specific questions.

Skipping to the Sub incident, he said: "On the notes in front of you, you will also see a detailed copy of the report we sent.

"We explained that the Radioactive leak was caused by a planted explosive charge placed on the top of the reactor cover. It was done by the Submarine senior crew, i.e., the Captain and his second in command.

"We determined that their official mission was likely a hoax, intended to create an attack on our crude oil supply and embarrass us by causing an environmental disaster that would bring condemnation on America.

"The real intention, however, was a plan to embarrass the CPRF president.

"We found that the actual orders for the incident came from several senior members of the CPRF, conspiring to unseat their president by planning a coup d'état. We also determined there was a connection between those conspirators and Iran.

"That was the gist of the report; we did, however, add a postscript concerning our findings."

Then turning to his notebook, he continued: "Separately, we indicated that we found several areas of concern that may or may not have had a direct connection with the Submarine Incident. And advised both the DOD and the DOS that we felt compelled to continue an investigation."

"Following the outline that Connie wrote, but that everybody has had input, we determined the following:

"The official course, as ordered by the CPRF Naval Operations, was to create an oil spill somewhere near the Bay of Valdez. It would show that the Russians were trying to create an environmental embarrassment that would force us to cut back on our oil production.

"We believe that the Submarine was to deposit multiple barrels of oil, anchored to the bottom, then set off by remote detonation. The destruction of the Submarine superseded these plans.

"From a report, given to us from MI-5 in the U.K., a North Sea oil drilling company was approached by Iran, with a proposal to ally with them in a plan to force Russia out of an existing competitive contract. The connection and proposal were made by an Iranian attaché to Switzerland, Darvish Abthai.

"Investigation showed that a direct connection existed between Abthai and Boris Kanski, CPRF senior aid to the Russian conspirators.

"An unconnected oil tank explosion in the UAE resulted in a joint U.S. and UAE exposure of sabotage by an individual from Yemen, named Ahmad Abd-El-Kader. He was connected with an Islamic cleric named Naseem Sargon in Azerbaijan, who had strong ties and connections with Iran.

"Concerns about these unrelated occurrences lead to a meeting and discussion with four unconnected business executives in New York City. They disclosed that reduced American need to import foreign oil had caused a change in global competition. This change created a significant drop in future market trade values, making us a target to unscrupulous investors. They felt the most probable physical target is the offshore drilling platforms that follow along the coastline in the Gulf of Mexico from Galveston, Texas, to Mobile, Alabama.

"Activity in Russia, confirmed by the U.S. CIA and MI-5 in the U.K., showed that the coup d'état conspiracy had been discovered by the CDRF president. The conspirator's aid, Boris Kanski, attempting to escape, was found and assassinated by the KGB.

"The next day, the Russian Sub's Captain and the second in command were killed by a firebomb, but not by the KGB. It was discovered that the bomb was created and placed by the same man from Yemen, Abd-El-Kader, who then fled to Baku, Azerbaijan.

"Further indications from assets in Moscow indicated that the coup d'état conspiracy had indeed been determined and the conspirators removed, disposition unknown.

"The North Sea Oil Company CEO contacted MI-5 to inform them of his decision not to accept the proposal from Iran. Communications between NSIU and MI-5 resulted in joint assets meeting together in Aberdeen, Scotland, with the oil company CEO. Access with American and U.K. assets in Russia determined a plot to destroy an oil rig in the North Sea.

"The U.K. Army Rangers under joint direction from NSIU and MI-5 stopped the attempt on a North Sea platform and arrested Abd-El-Kader. He is currently in U.K. custody."

"Recent activity throughout Iran, with several citizen demonstrations and riots, has had the effect of weakening the Iranian leadership. It is noted that the increase in global oil competition has strongly affected and decreased Iran's economy."

Harold stopped reading aloud, took a drink of water, and turned to the Admiral. He said: "That is what we know, is it enough?"

The Admiral sat quietly, looking around at all the faces, then said: "I believe that it is far more than what we were asked to find."

Then slowly looking around the room as everyone let it sink in, said: "However, as we all agreed, we kept finding different lines to follow. We did not then, nor, even now, know exactly where any of these roads would lead.

"I think we have done enough. I am sure there will be many questions, but that is for other departments to consider.

"Connie, would you and Harold please prepare a finished document in final report form, and then go ahead and submit it to both the DOD and the DOS."

As he stood up and with a relieved look on his face, he turned to everyone and said: "I want to thank you all; the process for this investigation has had a strong impact on all of us and has required many unique methods to determine a result. I hope that this is as strange as it ever gets. I expect we will have multiple clarification requests by the DOS and DOD; just do the best you can."

With that, he told them: "Meeting adjourned."

EPILOGUE

Friday, 10 May 2019
United States State Department
Washington D.C.

A t eleven o'clock Friday morning, Jane McCalla entered the State Department Pressroom and stepped up to the dais.

It had been several weeks since the last news reports. Secretary Weiss had been at trade and military negotiations in Japan and South Korea. Jane had accompanied him on this trip, along with three other aids.

The negotiations had gone well, and final preparations for the agreements were just about ready for the President to sign. The Secretary had conveyed an invitation to the two foreign leaders to visit the White House for the signing.

On Wednesday, when they got back to Washington, the final reports from NSIU and DOD were on their desks.

Jane spent several hours with Secretary Weiss discussing how much of the investigation results should be made public. The decision was easy; for the most part, there was nothing they needed to hold back.

The only problem was that there would still be questions regarding the Russian Submarine incident.

Secretary Weiss told her not to change everyone's opinion that it was an accident; Russia was, and would always be, faced with embarrassment by the incident. It had happened, and they needed to face up to it.

He advised her not even to mention it, and if asked, sidestep the subject by talking about America's improvement on its oil and fuel energy supplies.

She could explain that the United States economy had grown because of our improved energy supply. As a result, much of the previous global production from foreign countries had been forced to become more competitive, thus reducing foreign profits back down to more reasonable amounts.

There was no reason to add to world tensions by expounding on the Russian coup d'état attempt; quite simply, it had failed.

The Iranian attempts to alter the global crude oil market and thus change competition; was something else.

She could explain everything they found at the sabotaged oil tanks in Sharjah, including the request for United States assistance from the United Arab Emirates. It was always a good thing when the two countries could work so well together, and as a result, even the saboteur's identity and history were discovered.

She could also tell about the attempted attack on the North Sea oil platform. She could explain the close mutual actions and intelligence that resulted from the close cooperation of the NSIU and MI-5. She would give particular praise to the U.K. Army Rangers, who captured and detained the terrorist bomber.

When she got to the dais, she looked out at the reporters and said: "Good morning, I have much to tell you, but I am going to apologize and say that, with our tight schedule, I won't be able to answer any questions at this time."

Smiling to herself at the moans from the reporters, she began her report.

With her notebook open in front of her, she began with the meetings' results in the far east.

The actual report took her almost forty-five minutes to give, and in the end, she closed her notebook and said: "Thank you for your attention, and I hope you all have a good day!" She then turned and walked away with a hidden smile, amongst a plethora of questions that they shouted out at her back as she left the room.

CPSIA information can be obtained
at www.ICGtesting.com
Printed in the USA
LVHW091932271120
672850LV00004B/1114